CORALEE TAYLOR

I See You, Charlotte

Ties That Bind Series– Book One

*To all those who need a little extra
understanding, grace, and love as they
struggle with their inner demons... I see you.*

Contents

Content/Trigger Warning

This book contains scenes that may be triggering. Please refer to the content warnings below. This list may not be all-inclusive. Your mental health and safety is important. If you feel that any of the below items would harm you in any way, this is not the book for you. Read on safely, my friends.

Triggers may include:
  Drug Use
  Self-Harm, Suicide, or Suicidal Thoughts
  SA/SV/Dub-Con/Non-Con
  Abuse
  Death
  Mental Health
  OWD/OMD
  Miscommunication

Prologue

Do you ever wish someone would pop out of the ether and offer you the blue/red pill choice?

The blue pill would give you one hundred million dollars. Sounds like an easy choice, right?

All my problems could be solved with that amount of cash.

No more debt. No more boss. No more budgeting. No more driving the fucking piece of shit Honda that makes a God-awful grinding sound when I go more than 45 MPH. No more soul-sucking ex-wife.

I'd pay that crazy bitch a hefty sum to get the hell out of my life.

But me?

I'd be chilling on a beach somewhere, surrounded by beautiful senoritas and big-ass margaritas.

Fuck that would be the life, man.

Why would anyone even want to know what the red pill does?

It could make a big tittied, mute blonde with luscious lips appear and drop to her knees, ready to serve me for the rest of my life, and I would still pick the blue pill.

But what if the red pill could take me back... to her?

I've thought about Charlotte way too fucking often over the years. If I could go back to when she was mine, knowing what I know now, I would hold on so fucking tight and never let her go.

I still can't believe I lost her. I couldn't save her. I should have tried harder. Been better. Been whatever the fuck she needed. I knew I'd love that girl more than anyone else the moment I laid eyes on her back in high school.

Much to my ex's dismay, I was right. I've never met or loved anyone else like her.

I would give everything to go back. She thought no one knew, but I did. I saw her suffering; I just didn't know how to help.

What I would do to see her again, there's no limit.

Most people say they wouldn't go back in time to change things or back to a previous partner because they wouldn't be the person they are without going through the shit they endured following the split.

But I would. For her, I would.

I'd give up everything. I don't care that I would've never met the succubus that is my ex-wife, Melanie. She isn't even half the woman that Charlotte was, and though early in our relationship, I tried to convince her —and myself— otherwise, we both knew. Melanie would never and could never be Charlotte Belle Johnson.

It's funny how time can make things so clear. I know now exactly where things went wrong for us.

I would need one day. One fucking day to change everything and have the love of my life beside me.

One. Fucking. Day.

Chapter 1

Winter 2004

"What the fuck are you doing, Chad?!" I scream like a banshee in the middle of the crowded movie theater parking lot.

Why must all Chad's be complete douchebags? Is it a requirement at birth some sort of test-o-douche is performed, and those who score off the charts in douchery, well, congratulations, your name is now Chad.

Here I am, minding my own business, out seeing a movie, some Ben Affleck action flick, with my friend Stacy and her brother Dean.

Okay, her brother also happens to be my ex-boyfriend.

Unbeknownst to me, Chad had some unresolved beef with Dean and somehow found out we were in town.

Now here we are, standing in the middle of an ever-growing crowd. Chad bobs and weaves, giving his best MMA impression to get past me to assault my ex physically.

He's screaming obscenities and making threats, all the while looking at his brother for backup because, God forbid, he handles anything on his own.

I've had enough of this lame display of male posturing, and my anger has hit the roof.

"Back the fuck off, Chad." I hiss at him. And this motherfucker? He's so lost in his own douchery and rage that he shoves me, and I fall to the ground.

Now, I was raised to keep my hands to myself, but my dad made sure I knew that if someone put their hands on me, all bets were off. I saw red, and I may have blacked out there for a minute; the next thing I know, I'm storming away; and damn, does my right hand hurt.

* * *

"Charlotte!" an unfamiliar male voice rings out to me as I continue seething and cursing the male species in my head.

"Charlotte!"

Who in their right mind would address me at this moment of my —*probably a smidgen uncalled for*— adolescent rage?

I spin around, ready to lash out at he who dares speak to me.

"Who the fuck are *you*?!" I spit at this boy that I've never laid eyes on before.

He comes closer slowly. His hands raised in surrender as if approaching a feral animal, which, to be fair, I'm sure I'm doing a bang-up job of imitating.

The red haze that has dominated my field of vision for the last twenty minutes starts to fade, allowing me to see this boy in front of me.

This beautiful boy with long, inky black hair covering half of his sharply angled face.

Gray eyes pierce into the deepest part of my soul. The light shines off of the multiple silver chains adorning his corded neck. As my perusal reaches his large hands, I see they're decorated with several rings. I track a path to the frayed edges of a black hoodie that is sporting some death metal band insignia and down to his baggy black ripped rave pants.

He excites me. Flutters explode throughout my midsection when he latches those stormy eyes onto mine.

I've never really had a specific type, but I've never been drawn to this kind of vibe before.

Well, before today.

His brows soften as his hands lower to his side, "My name is Jason. I'm friends with Chad's brother, Adam. I saw what happened back there, and I wanted to make sure you were okay. Chad had no right to put you in the middle of that bullshit. Are you okay?"

Wait, *what?* I've been friends with Adam and Chad for years, but I'd never heard of this guy.

But something about his voice feels like a balm to my heated soul. Breathing is easier with each of his exhales.

I suck in a sharp inhale at the realization that I hadn't answered him.

I've just stared at him like a total idiot for the last few seconds. With a slight shake of my head, I finally find my words, "I'm okay, just really pissed off. I can't believe Chad. What a dick, it's like he didn't see me at all."

Jason's face kicks up into a sympathetic half-smile, which displays a dimple— a fucking dimple.

"He's such an asshole sometimes. I'm sorry you had to deal with it tonight. I hope he didn't ruin your weekend plans with your um... boyfriend?" he questions shyly.

I fail at holding back a very unladylike snort.

"He's not my boyfriend. Well, not anymore. We are just friends now. I'm good friends with his sister."

I could've sworn I saw a slight look of relief pass over his face.

"Well then, if you have no other pressing plans, would you like to come back to Adam's with me, and we'll get you some ice for that right hook, Laila Ali?" he chuckles.

Laila who? Did this asshole forget my name already?

He must have noticed the sour expression my face had taken on, and so he supplies, "You know, the boxer? Muhammad Ali's daughter? Because you hit Chad…. Never mind, it was supposed to be funny and make you smile."

Oh. I am truly an asshole sometimes.

"Of course, I know who Laila Ali is. I could use some chill tonight," I cock my brow at him pointedly. "But if I do this, I expect you to stay by my side at all times." I issue the decree like I am the damn Queen of England.

Maybe he will take that as me being too forward with him, so I immediately add, "To make sure Chad keeps his distance and I don't go for a TKO." I laugh at the continuation of his joke.

He nods his agreement, and silently, we fall into step and make our way the few blocks to Adam's.

Even over the thumping of some way too loud rap music, her voice sounds out above all other noise, "Girl, who the hell is that?"

My not-so-subtle bestie, Savannah, shouts at the sight of Jason and I walking into the house together. She simultaneously pulls me in the opposite direction as if heroically saving me from a would-be abductor.

I smile at Jason and mouth, "I'm sorry, I'll be right back." He shrugs and gives me a small wave as he turns to join a group of guys in the middle of a passionate discussion about their cars or something equally lame.

"Charlotte Belle Johnson, you better explain what you're doing here with that Gothic boy! I mean, he's kind of hot if you're into the scary serial killer type, I guess."

I love Savvy to pieces, but she cares a lot about her social status, and that extends to the type of people I hang out with as well.

I give her a quick rundown of how this evening went down, all the drama at the theater, and how Jason followed me to check and make sure I was okay. Her face softens at my explanation, and in true Savvy fashion, she was ready to take charge and help me forget all about it.

"Time to make some of my famous Screwdrivers, and when I see Chad, I'm kicking him straight in the nads!" she shouts to no one in particular while storming into the kitchen. The crowd easily parts way, like the Red Sea to Moses.

I see Jason from behind as I tap his shoulder with a finger; he turns to face me, and I smile gently while holding a cup in his direction,

"A peace offering for putting up with my no-filter-having best friend. I'm sorry if she offended you." I hoped he didn't want to write me off as a shallow girl who wasn't worth his time.

As he accepts the drink, he laughs, and God does his laugh light up his whole face. I had a feeling he didn't genuinely do it very often; we had that in common.

We both take a sip while holding each other's gaze. Tension seems to crackle like lightning in the air. As if it was some form of divine intervention —or punishment—Adam chooses this moment to stumble into both of us, arms slung over our shoulders, and slurs out something that resembles, "Well, aren't you two cute."

My face takes on a crimson hue as I choke on my drink and roll my eyes.

Savvy has been dating Adam on and off for the last year, and they are off at the moment, but still, I caught her eye from across the room and gave her a look to intervene.

She sashays over and ushers the three of us into another large group of people — yes! Thank you, Savvy.

After an hour or so of steady drinking and conversation, I excused myself to the restroom to splash some water on my face and check the current state of my hand.

I flex it out, stretching my fingers, and bring it back to a slight fist. It's still a little red, but the swelling has gone down.

As I returned to the room, my heart immediately fell into my stomach.

I see Jason sitting on the couch, laughing down at his lap. The very lap that my best friend's beautifully curled head is on. She flirtatiously gazes up at him, saying something I can't hear from here.

A scene flashes before my eyes of me walking over and sinking my hands into those bouncy curls and ripping her the fuck off of him.

I blink back my irrational homicidal daydream and step closer to the pair.

Why am I having this intense reaction? He is not mine; I have no claim to him. He can have whatever skank he wants lying on his lap.

Oh, stop it, Charlotte. This is your best friend. If they like each other, I will just have to put a smile on my face and deal with it. She's most likely just using him to make Adam jealous anyway.

Right?

Jason looks up at me and smiles brightly.

Why the fuck is he rubbing this in my face? What did I do to deserve this? He extends a hand in my direction, "Charlotte is back! Charlotte, why don't you help your friend up?" his eyes widen at me as if trying to tell me something.

"Seems she's had a few too many and needs to lie down somewhere."

Um, what is happening?

"Play with my hair, Jason," Savvy whines at him, and he shakes his head, seeming to grow weary of her drunken antics.

"No. You need to get up. Now."

Savvy dramatically sits up and flings herself into a standing — well swaying — position and makes her way over to the recliner.

Laughter fills Jason's eyes, and I raise a brow to him in challenge. I shoot a look at my drunk best friend and smile as wide as I can as I lay down to fill the space she just vacated.

Immediately Jason's hands go to my head, he starts gently threading his fingers through the strands.

"Hey! What the hell!" Savvy shouts and gives us her best pout.

Adam trips over his own feet to cross the room and sits on the arm of the recliner with Savvy.

"Don't worry, babe, I've got two free hands right here for you," she heaves a sigh. With a shrug and an eye roll, she lets him pet her head.

We all dissolve into giggles.

For now, the familiar cloud that hangs over my head has abated. I deserve some happiness, and despite how it started, this is the best night I've had in a long time.

Chapter 2

It didn't occur to me until five minutes before I had to leave my house that I might be seeing Jason at school today.

We had such a great time on Friday night. He made me laugh, and I felt so comfortable with him. We talked briefly about his being newer to the River View area; he attended the local middle school and is now a sophomore at River View High.

I hadn't realized he was younger than I was. I guess it makes sense that we haven't had any classes together since I was a junior.

I ensure my hair and make-up are perfect before heading out the door. Mom always drives me to school; it's our time to catch up on each other's lives. She works so much, and I am always so busy with school and hanging out with my friends that we don't spend time together like we used to.

My parents are amicably divorced and have been since I was ten. Dad lives in Alabama, where he grew up. When I was younger, I would spend the school year with my mom and summer break with my dad. Every major holiday, though, he flies up to us so we can all spend it together.

As we pull up to River View High, my nerves start to kick into high gear. I step out of the car with my school persona slipping into place— my alter ego, if you will.

I can't be myself here, not truly. No one really knows me except for Savvy— and she only gets maybe eighty percent.

When we were five years old, Shelly Devaney pulled my hair, and Savvy threw dirt in her face in my defense.

We've been besties from different testes ever since.

At school, I am outspoken; I'm friends with everyone, well, everyone that is considered important by the other narcissistic assholes who attend this school.

I have a reputation as a social butterfly with mega sass. At home, I am introverted, lonely, and a little hopeless.

I stride through the door, exuding all the confidence I can muster. Smiling and nodding at the proper people as I pass. Saying hello to the staff members I've managed to charm into thinking I am a worthwhile student.

I walk up the stairs to the main hallway, and I catch sight of shiny, onyx hair and black baggy rave pants to my right. I can only see Jason's handsome face until my attention is drawn to the hand firmly on his shoulder. A small dainty hand, with nails painted blue, that most definitely does not belong to the boy in question.

He has a girlfriend? How did that not come up on Friday? My smile falters for a moment before I get my emotions in check.

Our eyes meet, and I give him my best, platonic, polite smile with a small wave before walking past his group to head to my locker. My frosty acknowledgment disappointed him, but what did he expect me to do? Walk up to both of them and say, "Hey, thanks for letting me lay in your lap and flirt with you all night on Friday. Wild that you never mentioned a girlfriend."

Of course, she's beautiful too. A tall, raven-haired beauty with tanned, perfect skin. She might as well be a giant to my tiny 5'2 stature. Feeling like a dumb ass and now a little insecure, I quickly open my locker and take a deep breath. It's time to move on, Charlotte.

* * *

Classes move at a glacial pace, and I am more than ready for the lunch hour.

I join Savvy and a few of our regular crew at our lunch table. The large faux wood is full of bumps and bruises from students' past. I try to ignore the persistent sticky spot next to my elbow as we all mindlessly chat about the latest gossip, what happened over the weekend, and what everyone's plans are for the next weekend.

I'm pushing the tots on my plate around with my fork, lost in my thoughts, when I find myself engulfed in the scent of fresh rain and cedar wood. I can't help the smile that starts to form on my face. I knew before I even looked up that Jason sat down beside me.

"Hey, Charlotte. How was the rest of your weekend?" On the one hand, I'm glad he cared enough to come over here and strike up a conversation; on the other hand, I am confused about what he wants out of this.

Are we starting a friendship? Are we casual acquaintances? Are we just classmates who will wave and be cordial in the halls?

"It was pretty good, just chilled at home. How was yours?" Before he even has a chance to respond, I see a group of similarly dressed people to Jason heading our direction, and leading that group is the dark ice queen herself with a deep scowl on her face.

"Jason, we've been waiting for you at *our* table. We still need to finalize our after-school plans," she basically purrs that last part with some heavy innuendo.

Feeling like a third wheel in my own conversation, I decide it's time to go. As I go to stand up, Jason gently puts his hand on my forearm to stop me. "Jade, we have no after-school plans now or in the near future, and I didn't know I needed to check in with my friends before sitting elsewhere for lunch."

Ah, the raven-haired beauty has a name; of course, it would be a pretty name like Jade, and it goes so well with Jason. Jason and Jade, just *perfect*.

I can see their perfect life with their perfect house and perfect babies. Great, now I want to throw up. The scoff of an indignant girl brings me out of my daydream. "Whatever, we both know you'll call me before the week is over." With that gem lobbed in our direction, Jade takes her leave with her merry band of followers lagging close behind. What did she mean by that?

"Wow, she seems like a peach." I slap my hand over my mouth, with my eyes wide in horror. Sometimes I have no filter. "I'm sorry, that was a mean thing to say about your... friend?"

He looks exhausted. "Jade is my ex-girlfriend. I had hoped we could stay friends as we have the same friend group, and our parents are close, but she tends to put on this alpha-female display any time I so much as breathe in another female's direction. I'm sorry about that, and I will make our status very clear to her."

Does he think I can't handle her? I am Charlotte Belle Johnson, that beautiful bitch doesn't have anything on me.

I puff my chest out slightly, bristling at the thought that he might think I would cower to her.

"Jason, you don't need to apologize for someone else's

actions. If she has a problem, she's more than welcome to bring it up to my face. I don't have the time or patience to play games, so if that's what you're into, maybe it's best if you stick to your side of the cafeteria."

Okay, even though I know I'm overreacting to what just happened, and I logically know that he was just trying to clarify, I can't very well lose face now and back down, so I do the only thing I can do at this moment. I get up and walk away from him without a glance backward.

For the rest of the week, I avoid Jason. Jade scowls at me every chance she gets. I wonder just how clear he was with her since every time I see them, she's touching him in some sort of way while shooting victorious glances my way. Why does he let her do that? I don't have the energy to fight over a boy, and I won't be put in a position where I have to worry about my potential boyfriend and another girl. I know I am territorial anyway and have a reputation to uphold, so I decided on Friday that it's best just to let Jason and the idea of what could be float away.

I'm a fairly desirable girl. Several boys have shot their shot with me. I just don't want to settle for mediocre. Sure, I've dated a few boys, and while I don't consider myself to be so virtuous that I'm holding out for the perfect guy to give myself to, I don't want to look back and see myself handing my V card over to Tommy with the sloppy kisses and minute-man routine in the bedroom.

So far, I've yet to meet someone I have faith in to do it right and well. I can't imagine any guy at this school warming my bed.

Except for maybe the tall boy with the sharp jaw hair and piercing gray eyes. If only he were a possibility.

Chapter 3

"Savvy, do you think it's the wisest plan to go to this party tonight?" Out of the corner of my eye, I see the dramatic eye roll she gives. "Brock is a senior, and he is known for his wild parties and ever-revolving door of snatch." She ignores me and continues dressing for what is sure to be a regrettable night.

I've been feeling a little down lately, so Savvy has made it her mission to get me out of the house this weekend, making sure we look "hot as Hell"—her words, not mine.

Savvy is rocking a form-fitting gold dress that thrusts her girls right into her chin, making sure her best assets are proudly on display. It matches great with her mocha skin and shoulder-length chocolate brown, curly hair. Finishing the look out with a pair of black flats. Her 5'7 frame doesn't need any additional height.

While she begins to line her lashes, she motions me to the closet with her left hand.

As I thumb through the white plastic hangers, I come across a silky black, one-shoulder top with a zipper that goes diagonal across my breasts.

I admire the great-fitting top and pair it with my tightest boot-cut black jeans, which show off my best asset— my ass.

In order to fit all of this ass in the jeans, I had to lay down to pull the zipper up while my best friend laughed at me. After that breath-stealing fiasco, I tame my mid-back-length blonde locks, and we head to the Arctic entry.

Since it's wintertime, we grab big puffy jackets and warm boots — making sure to bring our cute footwear in Savvy's car to change when we get to the party.

"Charlie, tonight I plan to be one of those pieces of snatch." she waggles her eyebrows suggestively at me. "Brock can revolve my door as much as he wants to." The hussy winks at me.

I roll my eyes at her slut-tastic ways. My best friend is unapologetic about her lifestyle, and I admire that about her, but she doesn't always know when to reign it in.

Her dad passed away when she was little, and her mom has had a steady string of boyfriends coming in and out of their lives ever since.

So, I know where her issues come from; I'm not here to judge her. I support her as long as she's safe and happy.

* * *

A combination of smoke and stale beer invades my nostrils instantly as we walk into Brock's duplex. He lives with his two older brothers, who are in college, and they let him party as much as he wants to.

Savvy makes a beeline for the cooler in the kitchen and brings me back an unopened bottle of Russian Ice. I pop the top on my bottle and slowly sip while looking around to see who's here.

A few people are gathered on the couch in front of the TV, playing some car racing game. A few people are dry-humping on the makeshift dance floor in the middle of the room. Multiple conversations are happening in the kitchen, and a large group is playing a drinking game of passing cards with their mouths in the dining room.

Savvy hip checks me to get my attention and points her bottle toward the drinking game crew, where I see Brock. She flutters her lashes at me exaggeratedly and saunters over to join the game.

I take my Ice and walk around the party, chatting with a few people. My head is starting to pound from the amount of smoke, booze, and body odor floating around.

When I spot the sliding back door, I exhale a sigh of relief. I make my way towards the door, and once outside, I take a large breath while pointing my gaze skyward.

There's nothing like a crisp, clear Alaskan night. The big dipper is completely visible; my favorite constellation. This is when I feel the most at peace, in the still, quiet, and beautifully lit night.

I close my eyes briefly, taking in the fresh air when I get the hint of fresh rain and cedar wood. Jason.

Whiskey permeates the air as his hot, slurred breath floats my way, "Hey Charlotte, been a while. How have you been?"

If all I can be is his friend, I will take it. He's making the effort, so why shouldn't I reciprocate?

I turn to him and smile. "Hi Jason, yeah, it has been a minute. I'm good. How are things going with you?"

He slowly encroaches on my space more, "I'm okay, I guess." he tilts his head and gives me a cheesy grin, "Except there was this cool girl I was trying to get to know who has been ignoring me for a month and it hurts my feelings that she doesn't want to be my friend." he says with an exaggerated pout.

"Well, that cool girl is ready to be your friend and is sorry for being dramatic and avoiding you." I tease him right back. Our easy banter returning. We both laugh at our ridiculousness, and I start to shiver.

"Why don't we head inside? It's freezing out here." I hold my arms out with a flourish to usher him back inside. It's completely obvious that he's drunk, and I feel like it's my duty to make sure he makes it inside safely and doesn't freeze to death out here.

Once inside, Jason disappears towards the kitchen. I hang out watching the drinking game and laugh at Savvy every time she purposefully drops the card to lock lips with Brock, not that he's complaining.

It's been a little while, and Jason hasn't come back yet, so I go in search of him. I don't find him in the kitchen. I looked around the dining and living rooms, and I didn't see him there either, though if I was thinking this party was lacking adolescent grinding, I was wrong.

I don't even know why we come to these things. It's always an evening full of awkward and uncomfortable forced social interactions and cringe-worthy attempts at coolness.

My head turns in every direction to seek him out. The longer I go without finding him, the more my heart bangs relentlessly against my chest, and I find myself entertaining the wildest scenarios.

Did he find a girl to talk to that was more interesting than me? Or maybe he's hooking up with Jade upstairs, and I missed her coming in.

As I pass a closed door off of the kitchen when I hear a loud moan.

Oh God, he's fucking someone in the bathroom. I feel

tears threatening to prick my eyes. Immediately mad and disappointed at myself for having another jealous response to this boy I hardly know. I hear the moan again, but this time I'm certain it isn't a pleasurable moan— it's a painful one.

I knock lightly on the door, "Jason? It's Charlotte. Are you okay? Can I come in?"

I hear more unintelligible noises but no words; I take that as a yes and slowly open the door.

The first thing I notice is it is pitch black in the room; the second thing is something is blocking the door, so I can't open it enough to fully make it in the room. My hand skims the wall, running across a hand towel, but with no luck finding the light switch.

With concern, I apply more pressure to the door to force it open. I'm only met with loud, unsettling sounds. It dawns on me that the door is making contact with his body.

I squeeze myself inside the bathroom through the narrow opening, and my eyes start adjusting to the darkness. I can now make out Jason's silhouette, and he is lying on the floor with his head near the toilet.

I bend down and softly shake his shoulder, "Jason, can you hear me? Were you sick? What can I do to help?" The strongest urge to care for him floods through my body. He groans in response.

I grab the hand towel and wet it with cold water before sliding myself onto the floor by his head. As soon as our bodies touch, Jason wraps an arm around my thigh like a pillow and lays his head on my lap. I can tell he's losing the battle with consciousness, and I lay the cool towel on his forehead while smoothing his hair back.

His stuttered breathing begins to even out, and soon he's

falling asleep. I don't want him to be alone and choke on his vomit or something, so I'll sit here—in the dark, with the boy who makes me hope for more.

A few minutes or maybe hours go by, and the bathroom door is shoved open. The blinding overhead light is turned on, causing my eyes to squeeze tight to stave off blindness. When I peel them apart again, my very drunk best friend is peering at me with Brock over her shoulder.

"Jesus, Charlie! I've been looking everywhere for you. I had hoped you would find a boy to spend the night with, but this is not what I had in mind." She smirks at my position on the floor.

I shake my head at her and laugh, "Sav, I love you, but you need to lower your voice and turn that light off. As you can see, I am fine. I'll be out in a bit." she nods her understanding, flips off the light, and closes the door softly behind her.

"Charlotte."

"Charlotte, wake up."

"Charlotte!" My eyes snap open.

Smashing into me like a freight train, I realize that I am still in the bathroom with a now not-so-drunk Jason.

"Oh God, I don't even know how I fell asleep sitting up like this." he laughs, and it sounds a bit pained. "How are you feeling?"

"Well, I got too wasted, too quickly, and ended up puking my guts out in front of a very sweet girl who then sat in here with me all night instead of going out and having fun. So, I've been better." his response makes me giggle quietly.

"Thank you for taking care of me, Charlotte. You didn't have to do that, but I appreciate you looking out for me." I'm thankful for the dark room, so he can't see the blush that his words have caused.

"You're welcome," I say softly. "Now, let's go get some breakfast."

I go in search of my best friend, not at all surprised when I find her cozied up in Brock's bed. Thank God both are clothed. I definitely don't need to see either of their parts out in the open— again.

"Sav." No response.

"Savvy." Nothing.

"Savannah!" Barely a stir.

"Bitch wake up, his wife is home!" That gets her. Savvy shoots to her feet, her hair wild and mascara running down her rosy cheeks.

Frantically looking around for her purse and personal effects— including her underwear.

Laughing, I hand her the purse as she glares at me. "Time for food. Quit fucking around." I say tauntingly as I haul ass down the stairs before she can hit me. I find a smiling, sleepy, and mussed-looking Jason at the bottom of the stairs, looking up at me like I was his entire world. Maybe one day I could be.

The three of us walk to the little cafe across the street for some sustenance.

After our bellies are full of the world's best Spinach and Feta Quiche, we part ways to head home for a much-needed nap.

Chapter 4

Spring 2005

"I need my own car, Mom." I'm trying my best not to sound ungrateful, but all of these appointments I keep having to drop her off at are really adding up. It's really starting to cut into my social life.

"We can talk about you getting your own car. When you get a job and can support your gas usage, insurance, and, oh yeah, the car payment is pretty important. Unless you want all your friends to see the back of that pretty car being towed away for nonpayment while you stand there like a loser on the side of the street and lace up your Shoe-barus for the long walk home."

Mom thinks she's hilarious. Me? Not so much.

I fold my arms and pout while staring out the window as the medical plaza comes into view.

"I should be ready in two hours. Do not be late, or those Lambo-feeties will be getting really acquainted with the bike path when you lose driving privileges." She gets out of the driver's side and winks at me while I try to remove the scowl from my face and get out of the car. "Yes ma'am, two hours.

Got it."

* * *

As has become our routine over the last couple of months, I pull up to Jason's house, where I find him sitting on the steps waiting for me—writing in his notebook as usual. He is always writing in that thing, and he won't let me see inside it. I'm dying to know the contents.

I park and start to walk over to him. I can barely see the cord from the headphones, but as I get closer, I can hear the heavy metal blasting through them.

I take this moment to drink in the sight of him. We've gotten close in the last few months but are still just friends.

He hasn't hinted at wanting more, but he always wants to spend time with me. I haven't seen him with his friends much, and most of his time outside of school is spent with me. As I approach, he still hasn't acknowledged my presence, and I know this might be my chance to sneak a peek at the notebook.

I slowly approach from the side and crouch down, leaning slightly over his shoulder.

His stupid beautiful hair is blocking my view. I lean a little closer, stretching my neck to the side. I can almost make out some scribbles. If I could just reach out to move his hair a little.

Apparently, my brain and my hand are on the same wavelength. No sooner than I had the thought, I felt those silky strands on my fingers as I gently pulled his hair away. I felt the air whoosh through his hair, wafting his scent around my face as he slammed the notebook cover closed.

He turns to me over his shoulder with a smirk pasted on his gorgeous face. "Ugh, I thought I had you this time. Your reflexes are insane." I try to keep my face stern but can't seem to help returning his smile.

"Charlotte, I knew you were here the moment you pulled up."

"No way, you didn't even look up."

"I don't have to look up. I know when you are near me."

Um, what?

My heart starts to pick up its cadence. He nudges my shoulder playfully, "Are you ready to go?" I can't seem to manage words at the moment, so I nod and stand to head back to the car.

It's a warm spring day, so the windows are down, and the radio is playing some top 40s hits as we make our way up the winding road to the peak of Sky Ridge.

My favorite lookout spot. Well, lately, it has become *our* favorite lookout spot. We can see all of River View from up here. It's one of the only places I feel completely at peace.

I exit the car and close my eyes with my face towards the sun, taking a deep breath. I feel my world righting itself with every moment here.

Sighing contentedly, I open my eyes and spin around to find Jason with an amused smirk. "What?"

"Nothing. You just always do that. "

"Do what?"

"Act like it's the first real breath you've taken since the last time you were here." He flicks his head to the side to remove the strands dangling in front of his eyes and locks those stormy orbs onto mine before he continues, "I see you, Charlotte."

I had no idea that I did that. And the fact that he notices... wow.

Feeling slightly exposed, I shrug my shoulders and walk over to the picnic table I've claimed as my own with my trusty pen at the ready. I add a new doodle or word every time I'm up here. Last week's word was 'fake'.

That's how I feel. Fake.

He sits across from me, and we fall into an easy silence. He has his super top-secret notebook, and I have my sparkly green gel pen as I draw a three-dimensional "S" that starts with six lines to complete my word for today, 'sad'. I absentmindedly start humming an old song about biting the dust.

My pen goes flying as I'm startled by Jason hopping on top of the table, and I let out an unfortunate squeal.

My surprised facial expression melts into laughter as Jason stands above me, serenading me with the very song I was just humming.

He is giving the performance his all, complete with head rolls, toe taps, and gyrating hips. I laugh and smile so big that my face hurts, but I don't care.

At this moment, I feel real. I feel alive. I feel like me.

Time has gotten away from me, as it usually does when I am with Jason. I look down at my brick Nokia cell phone to check the time.

I was the first of my friends to get one and currently hold the high score on Snake. I am damn proud of this accomplishment.

"Shit! We've got to go. I have to pick up my mom," I touch the keypad to illuminate the screen again... "in fifteen minutes." We quickly gathered our things and started to make our way back to town.

We are in the middle of a lighthearted discussion about how snowboarding is most definitely different from skiing—his opinion— and that even though I'm the clumsiest person he's ever met, he's very confident in his ability to teach me.

"First of all, skiing is the Devil. I fail to see how snowboarding would be an improvement to that, and secondly…" my words fade away as I pull into his driveway and see a familiar tall, dark-haired female standing on his porch.

He offers nothing to me to acknowledge her presence at his home. We say our goodbyes as he exits the car.

As I make the ten-minute drive to the medical plaza, so many things are running through my mind.

Why was Jade there? Did he know she was coming? He didn't seem surprised. Did he purposely not say anything to me? I haven't seen them talking at school, do they talk secretly? I can't help but feel upset. I thought we were friends, and he trusted me, but how could he if he was keeping things from me?

I'm being ridiculous. It could be nothing. Maybe they have an assignment together. Maybe she's babysitting his little brother, Alex. Maybe she's meeting her parents there for dinner with Jason's family.

Maybe she's sticking her tongue down his throat at this very moment. *Maybe* he's walking her into his bedroom and touching her intimately. *Maybe* he forgot my existence the moment he was in her presence.

My mind is a whirlwind of images of Jade and Jason doing all the things in which I have no experience.

"Cutting it close, kiddo."

I hadn't even realized Mom was back in the car. "I like to live on the edge." I offer back sarcastically. "How did your appointment go?" I turn my head to look at her as she lifts a hoodie —that definitely doesn't belong to me— up with a cocked eyebrow.

"And who does this belong to, young lady?"

Shit. My mom has never said I couldn't date or hang out with boys, but I've always kept that part of my life private. She's never met anyone I was interested in— or briefly dated— and for good reason.

I know she would ask and say all the embarrassing parent stuff, and I want to keep Jason to myself for a little bit longer, so I lie.

"I ran Savvy to her new plaything's house; it must be his." I give her a shrug. "I'll give it back to her tomorrow at school." I can feel the rush of blood coming up my neck; I just hope she doesn't notice.

"Oh, that girl. She's such a free spirit. I feel sorry for the man who thinks he can tie her down one day."

My mom's amusement with my best friend makes me smile and forget my inner horror show montage of Jason and Jade. We head home to start dinner, one of our favorite things to do together.

Did she ever answer me about how her appointment went?

Chapter 5

"Don't even think about it, Charlie."

I am tired of having this conversation with Savvy for the hundredth time in the last week.

I haven't decided, but she's trying her hardest to sway me in her direction.

"Savvy, I just told him we could talk." I swipe my hand flatly through the air, "That's all. He didn't propose marriage. It's just a conversation. Chill out."

"It didn't work out the first time because Dean is a selfish prick, by the way. Why would you even want to give him another chance?"

I close my eyes, calling on all the calming elements of the universe to stop me from smacking my best friend right now.

I had hoped something would develop between Jason and me, but I've felt some distance since the day I saw Jade at his house a few weeks ago.

Two weeks ago, an ex-boyfriend contacted me, and we started talking. He has asked me to meet up with him and have a serious conversation about revisiting our relationship.

"We dated freshman year; neither of us was ready for a relationship, and we couldn't get on the same page." I pinch the bridge of my nose in frustration. "He's grown over the last two years, and so have I. I'm not sure if I want to be with him again, but I am willing to talk."

"And when is this life-changing conversation supposed to take place?"

"The day after tomorrow. I'm supposed to meet him at The Coffee Hut at 4 pm."

She nodded and let it go. Very un-Savvy-like.

Whatever, I have a ton of homework to do. I have no energy to entertain her shenanigans further, so I wave goodbye and head down the corridor to my study hall.

I can't wait for the day to be over; I need a beverage of an alcoholic nature and a nap.

* * *

Why do we have so many fucking essays in high school? Am I somehow going to be a better functioning member of society because I can fluff my way through a thousand words on the big earthquake of 1964?

I'm not a huge fan of public speaking, but I'd rather have an open class discussion about the topic than sit here and try to think of all the different words I can use to describe one event.

No one asked for my opinion on the matter, so here I am, trying to come up with yet another word synonymous with 'devastating'.

It's taken the better part of the school day, but I'm finally done with the rough draft of my essay. I have reread and restructured it three times. I'm mostly happy with it.

Well, happy enough. I have no will left in me to look through it a fourth time. I flip through the other assignments I have due next week. I've been distracted, so I know my weekend will mostly be spent locked away with my textbooks.

I glance at the clock, twenty more minutes to go.

By the time the end of class bell rings, my eyes are so fatigued that it takes a moment to focus before I walk out of the classroom.

I'm looking down at my binder, trying to put my essay safely away, when I crash into a body. The scent of cherries and almonds assaults my senses.

"Of course, it's you. Always in the way, aren't you, Charlotte?" Jade snarls at me.

"It was a fucking accident, Jade. Put your crazy away; it's not wanted or needed here."

She folds her sharp talons over her arms and crosses them over her chest, "How dare you. Who do you think you are?"

"Someone who has grown wary of your petty bullshit. Now if you'll excuse me..." I gesture down the hallway, "My ride is waiting to take me home."

A nasty smile makes its way across her face, and I just know her next words are meant to hurt.

"You know, you're right. I don't have time for this..." she brushes the imaginary lint off her skirt, "My ride is waiting too. Well, waiting to be ridden anyway." she laughs and looks at me over her shoulder as she walks away; she shouts, "I'll tell Jason you said 'Hi.'"

I lock down the emotions that threaten to cross my face as tight as I can so she can't see just how much her words crushed me.

My mind is reeling, and I need to get out of here.

I storm down the hallway looking everywhere. "Where the fuck is she?" I hiss to myself.

I just want to get Savvy and get the fuck away from this place. I scan the hall with our lockers, and I spot her chocolate curls and see her waving her hands dramatically to whoever she's talking to.

Hurry the fuck up bestie. Can't you use our best friend telepathy and tell that I can't be here anymore?

I sigh and close my eyes as I lean back against my locker, waiting for her to get done with her conversation down the hall. I hear a slam of a locker and snap my eyes open to look. That's when I see who Savvy is talking to.

Jason. And he doesn't look happy. He shoots a glare my way and turns in the other direction to storm off.

A smiling Savvy walks back to me like whatever weirdness that was didn't just happen.

"What the hell was that about?" I questioned. She walks past me and winks, "I don't know what you mean. Move your ass if you want a ride, I'm starving."

Fuck my life. Fuck Jade. And you know what? Fuck Jason too.

I think I'm ready to have this conversation with Dean in a couple of days.

Chapter 6

"Why do I have nothing to wear?" I whine as I throw yet another top over my shoulder.

I have gone through my wardrobe several times to find a cute — yet not desperate— outfit to wear for my coffee date with Dean today after school.

I pull out the black skirt again and hold it up against the white cropped sweater; this will do. I pull on my black tights and wear a pair of black chunky Mary Jane-style shoes. I look cute but studious.

Perfect. I curl my hair and give my make-up a little more attention than normal.

"Oh, sweet girl, you look beautiful. What's the occasion?" Mom asks as we both get our coffee into to-go cups.

"I just felt like I could use a little more armor today."

For as long as I can remember, my mom has told me whenever I felt down or sick to put extra effort into my outward appearance— for me, always just for me. She believes in the 'fake it until you make it' mindset, that more effort on the outside lends better armor for whatever is happening on the inside.

I walk into the bathroom to primp one last time before we head out for school.

A metallic scent lingers in the air, drawing my attention to the waste basket. Barely covered are several thoroughly filled pads.

Mom must be having a super heavy flow. I'll make sure she has her heating pad out, and I'll make dinner.

We both suffer from heavy periods and painful cramps, so I know she is not having a great time right now.

I make a mental note to make sure we have a good supply of Tylenol and her favorite noodle soup.

As we get ready to leave the house, a thought occurs to me. I'm always a week or so ahead of her in our cycles, and I haven't started my period yet.

Walking into school with my armor firmly in place, I smile brightly at my peers. I get several appreciative glances and a few catcalls.

I am starting to feel lighter already. My first few classes fly by, and my stomach grumbles just in time to remind me that lunch is up next.

"Hey lady, why don't we swing through the Burger Hut for lunch?" I question Savvy as we put our books away in our lockers.

"No can-do sunshine, I got plans for lunch."

"Since when?"

"Since Brock asked me to come to check out his baseball card collection," she says with an exaggerated waggle of her brows.

"Great, I guess I'll eat alone in the cafeteria like a loser." I know I'm being dramatic, but I need the extra shelter of my best friend today. I'm nervous about my meeting with Dean.

"I don't know, Charlie, something tells me you'll be just fine," she says cryptically as we part ways for the lunch hour.

I make my way to an unoccupied table off to the side with my prepackaged sandwich— which is utterly unappetizing.

I reach into my purse for my phone. Figure I might as well try to beat my current high score for Snake.

Heat engulfs me from behind as the smell of fresh rain and cedar wood reaches my nose.

We haven't spoken much lately. I've tried to keep my distance for my own selfish reasons. I was getting too attached, and I didn't know if I could just be his friend.

According to Jade's earlier statement, I made the right choice.

Without turning around and before he has a chance to speak, I feign boredom and say, "Jason, to what do I owe the pleasure?"

"Charlotte, would you take a walk with me?"

This is the most serious I've ever heard him be. I don't want to play games, and I'm tired of the emotional turbulence I feel in his company... but I am curious what he wants to say to me, so I nod and gather my things.

I follow slightly behind him down the hall before he opens the door to the pool area.

I'm immediately hit with a large whiff of chlorine. I blink my eyes quickly to stave off the tears that threaten to fall at the strong chemical.

"What are we doing here, Jason?" He doesn't answer me but gently takes my purse out of my hands to sit it on a pool chair. I don't think he's going to answer until he takes my hands into his, lowers his gaze to mine, and softly admits, "I made a mistake, Charlotte."

"What do you mean? What mistake?"

"I should've told you. I thought it was obvious, but I was wrong."

"What are you talking about? Tell me what?"

"I don't want you to be with anyone else; I can't watch that happen. I want you to be with me. I want you to be my girlfriend, Charlotte." he rushes out urgently.

Stunned, I stand simply blinking with my mouth gaping open and closed like a goldfish.

My brain is trying to catch up to the words he just said to me. He wants me? Like he wants to date me? Does that mean he wants to be with me exclusively?

I have so many questions, but the only one that comes out is, "What about Jade?"

He looks like I slapped him. "What *about* Jade? What does she have to do with you and me?"

"I don't want to be with you if you are hooking up with someone else. I won't be the other girl or one of many."

He shakes his head, seeming amused by my response. He is pissing me off, and I am gearing up to tear him a new one.

I start to pull my hand out of his when he gives me a mischievous grin as he tightens his grip, and the next thing I know, we are airborne.

The cold water envelops my body as we sink towards the bottom of the pool.

This boy has lost his goddamn mind. He just threw both of us into the pool. Fully clothed.

What. The. Fuck.

I sputter and swipe my hair off my face as we reach the surface. I must look like a drowned rat. I'm sure my make-up is running, and my hair is going in all directions, curls are long gone.

I'm going to kill him.

As he surfaces, he shakes his head back and forth in that hot guy way to dispel the excess water. He reaches out for me, and

I slap his hand away. We are both treading water; the force causes me to bob down again. His arm wraps around my now-exposed waist. He pulls me to his chest, and I immediately feel self-conscious. I must look terrible.

"Don't," he growls at me. *Don't what?* He answers like I voiced the question aloud. "You look beautiful. You always look beautiful, Sweets."

He swipes his thumbs under my eyes, no doubt removing the streaks of running eyeliner. His hand moves to the back of my neck, holding me in place with his stare.

His eyes are questioning. I give him a barely perceptible nod, and that's all he needs.

His lips slam against mine in a bruising kiss. I can't breathe. I don't want to breathe. I want more of this, of him.

I can't think. All I can do is feel. Jason is kissing me like I'm the air he needs to breathe.

His tongue lashes at the seam of my lips, begging for entry, which I grant him. He devours my mouth, and it's the hottest thing I've ever experienced.

We must have been moving because my feet can now touch the bottom of the shallow end, and without breaking apart, Jason backs me up to the edge of the pool. I'm completely lost in him; I couldn't tell you my own name at the moment.

He reluctantly pulls back but has both hands on the side of my face, gently forcing my gaze to his. "There is no one but you, Charlotte." his voice is thick with emotion, "There is nothing between Jade and me anymore, I promise you. You are all that I want. I will do whatever it takes to prove that to you." There's so much sincerity in his voice.

"Say yes, Sweets. Say you'll be my girlfriend. I need to hear the words."

he barely gets the last part of his sentence out. "Yes!" I rush out. "Yes, I will be your girlfriend."

He wraps his arms tightly around my waist, pulling up slightly so I wrap my legs around him and lock my arms around his neck.

We smile brightly at each other, and the moment seems to stretch on forever. He places a soft kiss on my lips as he leans his forehead against mine and closes his eyes, and softly exhales, "Thank fuck."

The loud bang of a door interrupts our intimate moment; it's then that I remember we are at school.

In the pool. Fully clothed.

My makeup is ruined, my hair is a mess, and the only other clothes I have are my extra gym sweatpants, school logo tee shirt, and sneakers. I don't even have an extra bra here.

Jason reluctantly puts me down. "Let's get out of here and get you into some dry clothes." All I can do is laugh as we make our way to the locker room area.

I rush to my gym locker and throw on a clean extra set of clothes. I feel uncomfortable knowing I have to go through the rest of the day without a bra or underwear, but it is what it is.

I wash all the makeup off my face and throw my hair into a messy bun before I make my way out of the locker room.

Jason is propped against the wall as I exit. He is in his normal clothes, but they are dry. Did he plan this? Crazy boy.

He frowns at me and slowly shakes his head. Oh God, I knew I didn't look great, but I didn't think I'd repulse him.

"This won't do Sweets."

"What's wrong?" I don't want to voice my insecurity, but I can't help it.

He doesn't answer me right away but starts digging in his

backpack. He pulls out a hoodie and walks towards me. "Arm's up."

I do without question as I am engulfed in warmth and all things Jason. That fresh rain and cedar wood scent making its way through my body, lighting up all my senses. I take a deep breath in. His fingers linger at the hem of the hoodie he just put on me.

He answers my unspoken question, "I could immediately tell that you didn't have a bra on, and there's no fucking way I'm letting you go through the rest of the day like that. I don't feel like getting into a fight today, and if my beautiful girlfriend walks around without a bra on, I know I would have to fuck someone up by the end of the day."

"Oh." I blink at him wide-eyed, stunned. He is so thoughtful and, at the same time, has a possessive streak that I've never seen before. I like it.

"Let's head to your locker so you aren't late for your next class."

We walk hand in hand through the cafeteria. I can't help but notice the hush that seems to fall over the room. There are eyes on us from all directions.

One of those sets of eyes belongs to a very smug-looking Savvy. I thought she went to Brock's for lunch.

She fucking winks at me, and my face scrunches up in confusion for just a moment before I realize. She knew. Now her earlier cryptic comment makes sense.

Jason squeezes my hand, pulling my attention back to him, and I smile up at him.

When we reach my locker, I grab the book I need for the next class and close the door. I turn to face my boyfriend. God, I love saying that. His arms cage me against the lockers, and he presses his mouth to mine; our bodies flush with one another, and a soft moan erupts from one of us.

He pulls back slowly, the effort that it takes written clearly on his face. He lightly tucks a loose strand of my hair behind my ear.

"I can't believe I get to kiss Charlotte Johnson," he says with a bemused smile.

"Any time you want. Boyfriend." I respond cheekily.

I lean up on my tiptoes to give him another quick kiss before we part for class. I watch his retreating back and bring my fingers up to trace my lips, feeling the lingering sensation of his lips on mine.

I smile to myself as I turn around to head to class when I see one more pair of eyes watching me, and with her expression, she also saw the whole interaction Jason and I just had.

Jade's mouth is agape in clear astonishment, and she looks fucking furious. I feel a little smug about it. I'm tired of her trying to intimidate me and lay claim to a boy who clearly doesn't want her.

What's the expression... When they go low, we go high? Be the bigger person? Treat others as you would want to be treated? Well fuck all of that.

If Jade wants to be bitchy and petty, then that's what she'll get in return.

"Jade. Honey, close that mouth or the rest of the male population will know it's ready for the next dick. I can smell your desperation from here."

The classmates around give a chorus of 'Oohs and Ahs' as I give her my most saccharine smile and stroll past her.

Checkmate bitch.

Chapter 7

Last day of School Before Summer Break, 2005

"Last day of school bitches! We are officially seniors!" Savvy shouts to the large group of students gathering in the cafeteria.

She's met with hollers and cheers.

One more school year to go. Then what? I haven't been worried about the future at all.

My whole world has revolved around the boy who has stolen my breath and maybe my heart over the last three months.

Jason and I have become that sickly sweet couple that other people hate to be around. We are always touching or kissing.

We particularly like kissing, and our attention never strays from each other for long.

Every day after school, we head to his house and spend the free hour we have making out and rubbing ourselves against one another before Alex comes home.

We haven't gone further than that. He seems to be almost resistant to taking it to the next level.

To be honest, I'm a little self-conscious about it. I don't think I'm quite ready to take things further, but aren't boys usually the ones pushing for sex? I think he knows I'm a virgin; we haven't discussed it openly, though.

Maybe my inexperience is what stops him, and he finds it to be a turn-off. We need to talk about it; I can't keep making wild assumptions.

Soon. We'll talk about it soon.

Savvy enthusiastically high-fives me—way too hard— but I don't want to dampen her happiness, so I give her equal effort back.

"Seniors! We will rule the school with an iron fist, and the peasants in the lower classes will bow to our reign!" I respond with a dramatic, terrible attempt at a British accent, and it makes my bestie grin.

Mission accomplished.

Thick arms wrap around my waist, and a chuckle is breathed into my neck from behind. "My girlfriend, the Queen. You're my Queen, so it makes sense that you'd be the whole school's as well."

"What does that make you? King? Prince? Or maybe concubine? Court Jester? I think Mastress Jason has a nice ring to it, what do you think?"

He gives me his response in the form of a bite to the side of my neck as he growls in my ear, "You can call me whatever you want as long as you call me yours." I laugh as he licks the sting out of his bite. "Always."

"Let's get out of here before I get cited for PDA. Alex is going to a friend's house after school, so we have my house all to ourselves for a few hours," he whispers in my ear, hot breath causing shivers to run down my spine and the area between my thighs to fill with warmth.

"Savvy!" I yell loud enough to capture her attention.

"What?"

"Let's go, you've addressed the masses enough today, and everyone is aware that you will be their ruler next year, or they will suffer the wrath of The Supreme Queen Bitch."

"I don't know, Charlie; some of these savages look like they haven't quite gotten on board."

I roll my eyes so hard at her that I'm almost afraid they will never come back to their rightful place.

A chair next to me catches my eye. I drag it over and climb on top.

Cupping my mouth, I address the large group of mixed classes, "Hello, little people of River View High! I am but a simple lady-in-waiting, but I would like to inform you that you stand in the presence of Queen Savvy Mitchell." I give a little bow of my head in her direction. "Rightful heir to the senior throne, leader of the cheers, and designer of the yearbooks. Matriarch to the beloved River View Colts Pep Squad. Bow to your Queen."

I thrust my fist in the air like I'm leading a charge into battle. "Long may she reign!"

I hop down and loop one arm through Savvy's and one arm through Jason's and lead us to the doors with the sounds of cheers and laughter sounding behind us.

Savvy, being the shameless floozy she is, waved her hand in a cupped manner fit for a true queen, "Goodbye, my loyal subjects, see you all in the fall!" she shouts over her shoulder as the three of us dissolve into laughter while making our way to her car.

The tension in the car is ratcheting up to an intense level.

Jason has been absentmindedly rubbing circles on my inner thigh with his fingers for the last ten minutes.

The slight sensation is driving me crazy. This boy makes me want things I've never wanted before. I want his fingers rubbing circles in other, more intimate places.

The familiar house comes into view, and I feel the squeeze of his large hand on my thigh.

As we came to a stop, I finally let out the breath I'd been holding in. I know we are about to embark on some new territory, and I am equally terrified but so very excited.

"K' bye!" is all I offer my best friend as I throw the back door open, clearly in a rush.

"You kids have fun; don't do anything I wouldn't do. Actually, you know what? Maybe you should!" she cackles as she pulls out of the driveway.

Oh God. Get it together, Charlotte. It's just sex.

Chapter 8

Jason walks in front of me, holding my hand. The walk to his bedroom has every butterfly that resides in my stomach taking flight all at once.

I've been alone with him plenty of times; I don't know why I'm so nervous now.

I want this. I want him. I'm comfortable with him, and it feels right.

"Sweets, I can hear you overthinking from here. We don't have to do anything you don't want to. This is all on your timeline."

Some of the tension in my shoulders releases with his reassuring words.

We walk into his room, and suddenly, I don't know what to do with my hands. I feel like I normally have a hand in my back pocket or maybe in my coat pocket. Who came up with the idea of pockets? They are so handy and useful. I can't imagine not having this little area to put my hands and important things like my Strawberry Kiwi lip gloss or wallet.

Oh my God. Why am I thinking about pockets right now?

Jason's hands come over my shoulders to slide to the lapels of my coat as he slowly removes it. I take a deep breath. His hands then slide around my middle as he pulls me back into his chest with his mouth to my ear.

"What are you thinking about now, beautiful girl?"

"Pockets." I blurt out. I really need to work on my word filtering.

He barks out a laugh, "Charlotte, you are the most intriguing girl I've ever met. I love the way your brain works. You are so random," he presses a kiss to the side of my neck.

"And smart," *Kiss.*

"And funny," *Kiss.*

"And kind," *Kiss.*

"And Sexy." He sucks on the spot just below my ear, giving it a slight nibble. A moan works its way up my throat before I can stop it.

Jason comes to stand in front of me and slowly backs me up to the edge of his bed. His hands find the hem of my shirt as he skims my hot skin with his calloused fingers. The sensation gives me goosebumps all over. I pull him forward roughly for a hungry kiss as I push my own hands up his shirt to rest on his hard chest. He pulls back enough to slightly pull on the hem of my shirt, his eyebrows raised in question.

I nod my head vigorously. He rips it over my head so fast that my vision blurs for a moment. He stands back to take in my partially undressed state. He licks his lips. "Perfect." And then his mouth is back on mine. Our tongues competing for dominance, I bite his bottom lip and then suck it into my mouth. He growls at me and slams our bodies together. I can feel his hardness pressing up against me, and it spurs me on further. I feel his hand rising to my back and stopping close to my bra clasp. I don't want him to hesitate, so I reach back and put his fingers on the clasp, silently giving my approval. He takes it immediately and removes my bra.

His hands caress my hips as his stormy eyes scan my body up and down. I take his hand and lean back on the bed, bringing him with me. He settles on the right side of me with his hands roaming my soft middle. "Touch me, please," I beg.

"Where do you want me to touch you, Sweets?"

"Here." I take his right hand and place it on top of my left breast.

He takes hold of it immediately, gently massaging it as he leans in to capture my lips again. I want to feel the heat of his body on mine, so I reach down to remove his shirt. His hands start to move down my chest and stop at the top of my jeans. "Can I touch you here, baby?"

I nod.

"I need the words, Charlotte. Tell me what you want."

"Yes, I want you to touch me there."

He unbuttons my jeans and brings them down my legs slowly enough to cause my anticipation to skyrocket.

Thank God I wore the cute black thong today.

My hips try to jump off the bed when I feel his lips place a hot kiss to my thigh as his hands go to my hip bones, holding me in place.

He trails kisses all the way back up to my mouth as his hands descend to the front of my panties and begins to rub me slowly while devouring my mouth and gradually picking up speed until I feel the beginnings of an orgasm.

I embarrassingly pant into his mouth and squeeze my eyes shut as he thrusts a finger inside of me, and a ripple of white-hot pleasure takes over my core. "Good girl," he whispers to me as he slows his rubs down to milk every ounce of pleasure out of me.

Still blinded by the effects of my pleasure, I reach down to feel his hardness over his pants. "Off," I command.

He doesn't make me ask twice. "Boxers, too," I add.

This is the time when he would usually make a sarcastic remark about me being bossy or make a lewd dominatrix comment, but he is laser-focused on our naked bodies. I want to be seductive and alluring, but I have zero patience, so as he works on his clothes, I take the opportunity to wiggle out of my panties, too.

His breath catches at my exposed skin, and his gray eyes turn dark and stormy. "Are you sure about this, Charlotte?"

I don't like the concern in his voice. I know this is what I want, and I want it with him.

"I'm positive, Jason. I know we haven't really talked about it…" My hands twist nervously in my lap as my lashes flutter, trying to avoid his gaze, "but I couldn't imagine my first time with anyone else. I trust you. I want you. I'm just nervous… I don't want to disappoint you by not measuring up to your previous experiences."

He laughs softly and shakes his head while wrapping his hand gently around the side of my face making sure I'm looking him straight in the eyes, "I have no doubt that you and I coming together in this way is going to be nothing short of amazing. I want *you*. I trust *you*. And I'm also nervous. And baby?"

"Yeah?" I breathlessly ask.

"There is no experience to measure against. And I couldn't imagine *my* first time with anyone other than you, beautiful girl."

What? What the fuck did he just say? *He's a virgin?* I assumed he had done it before, at least with Jade. Oh my God. This is…

Perfect. This is everything.

This feels right. I smile the biggest smile I can and pull him down to me, kissing him with vigor. I hear the crinkle sound of the condom wrapper. I have no doubts at this moment. I'm ready. Jason slides the condom on and situates himself in between my legs, with one last questioning gaze, both of us giving slight nods to each other. He slowly breaks the last barrier between us.

Once the pain subsides, he picks up the pace. Exhilarated with our coming together, I'm feeling things I couldn't even imagine were possible throughout my body. We are both lost in the pleasure of each other as we hit our peak together. He slows to a stop and looks at me with a heartfelt expression on his handsome face.

"I see you."

Chapter 9

Jason –and Jade– decided to take summer school courses to gain credits for early graduation. Which means my summer days have been entirely lackluster and explains my current state of resident couch potato.

"Charlotte honey, are you planning to put on regular clothes today?" my mom asks with laughter in her voice, looking at my disheveled state on the sofa.

"I haven't made up my mind yet. I'm just too involved in finding out who Becky's baby daddy is and whether she will pass the lie detector test or not." I stretch languidly against the couch when something soft smacks me right in the face.

"What the hell!" I shout.

"Get your grubby butt in the shower Lola. I can smell you from here," she says in her stern mom voice while trying to cover up her laughter. She always uses her special nickname for me when she's in a playful mood. It's always been helpful for me to distinguish when I'm actually in trouble or not.

After a few more episodes, I'm starving and leave my trash TV show long enough to venture to the kitchen.

Mom is pacing the back porch with her phone pressed tightly to her ear. Her voice is too low for me to make out the conversation, but I can see tear marks. She turns, and we make eye contact; she shrugs her shoulders and rolls her eyes while letting out a slight huff of laughter before she spins back around, continuing her conversation.

My phone dings with a new text message.

Jason: Hey Sweets, I have to go to dinner tonight with the fam. I'll hit you up when I get home.

Ugh. Another dinner. I swear, sometimes I think they have all these "special" dinners just to keep us apart. Jason's dad is not my biggest fan. I'm not sure why he seems to have some animosity towards me, but I can feel it, even if Jason tells me I'm crazy.

Me: Aw, okay, babes. Have fun. TTYL.

Well, there goes my evening... Again...

After spending my day doing nothing important, I lay in bed trying to convince myself to stop looking at my phone every five seconds. Jason didn't text me back.

Did he forget? Did his phone die? Are they still at dinner? I glance at my alarm clock. It's 11:30 pm. So not still at dinner then. How did I get this pathetic? It's Friday night; I am a— soon to be— eighteen-year-old, and I'm acting like an old lady. Fuck that, I pull out my phone and shoot a text to Savvy.

Me: Wat r u doin?

She replies almost instantly.

Savs: Daveeee gaung paqty! Bock invit3 me

Well, it certainly seems like my best friend has been partaking in alcoholic beverages this evening.

Me: U didn't think to tell me about this party?

Savs: I thought u be wif the Gothic boi!

I roll my eyes; Savvy loves to call Jason "that Gothic boy we adopted" since he showed up at our lunch table one day and just never left.

Me: Nah, he had dinner w/ his fam... Ya know, we aren't ALWAYS together. It'd be nice if my best friend involved me when she gets invited to exclusive parties.

Savs: OMG Charlie I am soooooooo sorry I dint mean to leave you oout I terribly best friend the worst!

I laugh out loud at her drunken dramatics. I don't want to push it further and ruin her night, so I decide not to tease her. Not tonight, at least. One of us should be having a good time.

Me: U are the bestest friend! I luv u, have a gr8 night, be safe! Call me 2morrow.

Savs: I ksdjpfioweh YOU!!!!!!!

I take that as Savvy drunk speak to say she loves me too. I lay down and close my eyes tight.

My chest is tight, like a weight resting on my diaphragm. I take a deep breath and will it to go away. When that fails, I try counting to one hundred in my head.

When this feeling creeps in, I want to crawl out of my skin. It's like being locked in place; the straight jacket tightens every few seconds, and I'm moments away from losing breath entirely.

I want to go up to Sky Ridge— my happy place, where my thoughts vanish and my lungs can fill. It's late now, and I doubt Mom would be very happy with me driving around with no purpose.

I check my phone one last time, nothing new. So, I send one last message to my boyfriend.

Me: Still haven't heard from you, hope you had a good night. I'm going 2 bed. TTYL?

I lay down and pray for sleep to find me soon.

Chapter 10

I hate that the first thing I do when I wake up is check my phone. I hate it even more that I have no new notifications waiting for me.

Now, I'm starting to get mad. If he is too busy for me, then I need to find something else to fill my time.

I gather some clean jeans and a light pink cropped tank to throw on after my shower.

"I'm heading over to Savvy's. I'll be back later! Call if you need anything." I shout to my mom as I head to her car. As long as I keep my grades respectable, she has agreed that I can use the car on the weekends at my leisure unless she informs me of her need ahead of time.

I know my bestie will be rocking a hell of a hangover, so I decide to be nice and grab us two mochas from the Coffee Hut. The tightness in my chest from last night seems to have faded. The sun is shining, there are barely any clouds in the sky, it's a beautiful morning. I pull up to the cozy duplex that Savvy and her mom rent.

We've always lived within three minutes of each other; Mary is basically my second mom. I haven't been a guest here in a really long time. I knock and laugh as I hear a curse on the other side of the door. It swings open, and I see a beautiful, if not a bit hungover, older version of my best friend.

Mary Mitchell is probably the youngest of all my friends' moms.

She had Savvy when she was seventeen. They basically grew up together. Mary gets looks from other moms and judgments on her image and her young age of thirty-four.

She sees that it's me. I give her a wide grin and hand her my mocha. It's my sacrifice, so I may live to see another day. She accepts the coffee with a grunt as she scurries away back to the dark cave she crawled out of.

As I make my way to Savvy's bedroom, I can hear the sawing of logs before I even open the door. It's dark and smells like dryer sheets, vodka, and a hint of vomit.

I hold my gag in as I kick the exposed foot hanging off the bed. No reaction. I waft the coffee close to her face. Nothing. I run my finger gently between her brows; she crinkles them but still doesn't wake up. I plop down beside her and see her phone tight in her grip, partially under the pillow. I slowly reach over her to pull her phone away; it starts to come easily. I almost have it. "I don't fucking think so, Charls," her phone is ripped out of my grip.

"And how are we feeling this morning?" I ask with a knowing smirk.

"Like I make poor fucking life choices sometimes, and I have an annoying best friend who's on the verge of getting a karate chop to the throat." she rasps as she reaches for the caffeinated lifeline.

Well, okay then. I hand her the coffee and back away. Letting the beast stir at her own pace is in the best interest of my personal safety.

"So, what went down last night at Dave's party?" I ask;

something dramatic always happens at his parties.

"Oh my God, Charls, you missed it! Stephanie, with the weird eyebrows, showed up in a freaking mini dress looking like La Femme Nikkita with her blonde hair slicked back, and guess who she was caught grinding on?"

"Who?!" I demand.

"Josh-mother fucking-Hilston!" she whisper shouts.

"*What*?! No fucking way. Was Lisa there?" Lisa is Josh's longtime girlfriend, known for her crazy jealousy and explosive fights with him.

"She walked in just as Stephanie was smashing her badonkadonk into Josh's crotch, and he had his hands sliding up the front of her dress!"

Oh shit.

"What did crazy pants do?" I'm invested now.

"She marched over to them and yanked Steph by her hair away from Josh and jabbed her in the throat with the side of her hand!" she inserts a dramatic pause as she sips her coffee, "While Steph was bent over trying to breathe through the choking, Josh tried to slink away like nothing happened. Lisa kicked him right in the fucking nuts! And the kicker— yes, that's a pun— he was hard when she kicked him." she slaps my thigh in earnest.

"Charls, he went down like a goddamn sack of potatoes. It was the funniest shit I've ever seen."

"So, is it safe to say she broke up with him?" I ask.

"That crazy bitch was sitting on his lap with a bag of ice and her tongue in his ear an hour later."

We both lose it at this point. I almost fall off the bed laughing so hard, and Savvy has tears running down her cheeks.

"Jesus H. Christ, some people's kids." I sigh.

Chapter 11

The past few weeks crawled by, but finally, we are going back to school on Monday. Most kids my age are dreading the start of a new school year. I can't wait. I am so ready to graduate and start the next chapter of my life.

My parents and I have been discussing my next steps. I think I want to take a gap year from college and get some work experience.

I've been leaning toward wanting to enter a nursing program, but my mom suggested I take on an entry-level job at the hospital to get a feel for the environment.

I see myself working with kids. It fills my heart with warmth to imagine being the one to put smiles on their smushy little faces.

There are quite a few reputable schools with nursing programs around the country. My dad has suggested that I come visit him and check out Auburn University's campus as a possibility. While I'm keeping my options open, it's something to consider, I've never lived outside of Alaska.

As our Friday tradition has been, Jason, Savvy, and I are meeting some people at Tim's Creek.

Tim's Creek is a trailhead at the base of Tiger Mountain. Once you surpass the trailhead, a beautiful flowing river guides you all the way to a breathtaking glacier, it is a highly popular area for parties, mainly because you have to mud-bog back to it.

If you don't have a huntin' buggy, a 4-wheeler, dirt bike, or vehicle with incredible mud tires and 4WD, you likely aren't making it back to the clearing spots, which means it is very difficult for the Troopers to shut down our little gatherings.

"Fuck!" my ever-graceful bestie shouts as she loses her footing in the soft silt.

"Chillax Savs, it's just a little dirt," I say while trying to cover my laughter.

My platform sneakers are making it through just fine, and to be fair, I tried to warn her. I grab her arm to keep her from face-planting into the ground and loop my arm through hers as we make our way through the dense trees we walked through to pee.

"I think I got some on my hand!" she whines sarcastically while wiping her damp hand on my bare shoulder.

"What the hell! Fucking gross, Savannah!" I scream and push her away from me, delighting in her wobbly stance in the pliable dirt. She chuckles and winks at me as she heads off to entertain her adoring fans from the cheer team. Bleh, no thanks.

Fire dances along the trees, lighting the path ahead. Music filters through the brush; something about not practicing Santeria and not having a crystal ball.

I lift the red cup to my lips and hum along. Finding a car to lean against, I close my eyes and absorb the warmth from the fire and the burn of my favorite whiskey going down my throat.

My body sways side to side along with the beat. A warm hand on my shoulder startles me out of my groove. My eyes meet a pair of very bloodshot ones peering back at me.

"Angel! My girl! How the hell have you been?" his full cup is sloshing over the edge. I jut my hip to the side to avoid getting doused in booze. "I haven't seen you in forever. Are you still living in River View? I don't think I've seen you in like five years. I always liked you, you know. I know you would never have given me a chance back then. Did you know I play football now? I'm a quarterback. " Michael slurs out to me in a rush with barely a breath taken.

I can't help but giggle at the boy in front of me. We grew up in the same neighborhood and played outside together until all hours of the night. His family moved to the lower forty-eight when we were in middle school, but he still has family locally, so he must be here visiting.

"Mikey! I'll take that, thank you." I take the red cup that he's clearly had way too much of out of his hands and sit it on the hood behind me. I lean out to give him a friendly hug. To which he lingers a little too long, and his hands slide a little too low.

A throat clears, and I whip my head in its direction, "I don't know who the fuck you are, but I suggest you remove your hands from my girlfriend's ass before I remove them from your body." he growls from my side.

I smile cheekily. I secretly love it when Jason's possessive side comes out.

"Babes! This is my childhood friend, Mikey." with a pointed look at my boyfriend, I lean into his ear and place a kiss right behind it. "Please be nice, he's hammered," I whisper.

Mikey looks Jason up and down like he's gauging whether he can take him down or not.

He absolutely cannot.

My boyfriend may be a sweetheart to me, but he is very

intimidating to the rest of the population with his 6'2 height, broad shoulders and what Savs like to call his 'serial killer blank expression'.

I don't see it, but I can clearly tell Mikey has decided not to chance it and to turn on the charm.

"Hey, friend! I was just catching up with my Angel here."

Oh God, shut up, Mikey. Does he have a death wish? Before Jason can move a muscle, I interject with a laugh, "I saved him from a rabid squirrel *one* time on the playground in elementary school. He's called me his Angel ever since."

"Cute." my boyfriend gruffly responds.

It's time to defuse the tension and get back to having a good time.

"Mikey, it was great to see you. Give my love to your momma. I have to show Jason, a thing... Over there... Away from everyone else." I wave and give him a wink as I grab Jason's arm and lead him away.

I immediately push Jason against the nearest tree once we're out of sight; he looks at me with surprise but is thoroughly entertained by the events.

"Do we need to talk about what just happened?" he asks with a smirk.

I shake my head. "Sorry, boyfriend, I'm all talked out. If you want to talk to someone, I can send you back to the party."

"Well... I don't know why else you would bring me over here, all alone, in the dark, if not to have some super-secret conversation."

I step on tippy toes and press a chaste kiss to his jawline, "Oh, no idea, hm? None at all?"

"I have no clue. I'm a good boy with only pure thoughts." he shrugs casually, but the restraint in his fisted hands gives him away.

I enjoy watching the smile slide off his face, and his eyes widen when he feels my hand on this belt.

"Nothing about to happen in these woods is pure, baby. Now, kiss me."

Chapter 12

I can't breathe. Blackness engulfs everything around me. I stretch my hand out and feel nothing but moist air. There are no discernible noises.

Icy hands are making their way into my chest and squeezing the life force out of me. This is how I die, alone in the dark, quiet, cold emptiness.

A garbled noise fills the air, and I can't quite tell what it is. Between the blood rushing to my ears and my internal panic, I can't focus on one specific thing.

A loud banging sounds around me. These must be the hounds of Hell arriving to drag me into the abyss. I start kicking my legs and punching the air in front of me, trying desperately to protect myself.

Finally, my voice returns, and I thrust my fists to my side, "Leave me the fuck alone!" I howl into the void.

The banging increases. I cover my ears with my hands as a loud roar has me whipping my head in all directions.

Squinting, I can see a bit of light off to the side, and my legs begin to carry me closer. It's like a spotlight on the blackness surrounding me.

As I near the light, I can just make out a shape on the ground. What is that? My steps slightly falter. I begin chewing my bottom lip. Is that a person? Black and green plaid catches my attention; legs come out of the skirt, and dark patches cover the visible skin. Is that blood?

A heavy metallic scent permeates the air around me. Kneeling close to the form—a girl— and she's covered in blood. Putting my hand to the closest puddle, it's warm.

"Hey, are you okay?" I barely recognize my shaky voice. The girl doesn't move. I can't see her face. Her hair is an unrecognizable color due to the amount of vital fluid enveloping her body.

"Miss, can you hear me?" I try again

The banging is getting louder. Closer.

My hands are shaking uncontrollably as I slowly reach out towards the girl. "Please. Please. Please." I don't know what I'm begging for.

The pounding is getting closer. I hold my breath as I grab onto a bony shoulder. "Please. Please. Please." I chant as I press down to roll the girl towards me.

I feel the warm liquid seeping into my jeans through my knees, which are pressed to the ground. The acrid metallic smell is burning my nose. I force myself to swallow the saliva filling my mouth, and I try desperately to hold in the acid that begs to make its way up my throat.

Her body rolls in my direction, the spotlight making her blood-soaked hair glow. I can see a few blonde strands unaffected by the dark fluid. Fuck. I try to focus on whether I can hear or see her breathing. There's nothing. I try to shake out the tremble in my hand as I reach forward to move the bloody strands out of her face.

"Miss?" I try again.

The rhythmic pounding is getting closer still—clearer— as my fingertips reach her hair. I gently swipe it aside, revealing the milky, lifeless chocolate-brown eyes that seem to look straight through me.

Faintly, I hear my name being shouted from somewhere behind me. Charlotte! *But I can't look away.* Charlotte! *My name is getting more distinct, but I can't look away.* Charlotte! *Not from the hypnotic gaze that's steadily trained on my face.*

"Charlotte!" *The voice is louder.*

"Do you hear me?" *Yes, I do.*

"Open this door now before I break the fucking thing down!" *Wait, what?*

My arm twitches as though my muscles are fighting to wake up. I know I should move. Run. Get away.

"Lola! Now!" *Come on, Charlotte, move.*

I inhale shakily as I slowly pull my fingers back. My eyes still glued to that vacant stare. I recognize the opaque blankness.

I should recognize them; I've seen those eyes every day for the last seventeen years.

This is no random girl lying here covered in blood.

This girl... is me.

My eyes fly open, and I gasp for air as the pounding continues on my bedroom door. "I'm up!" I shout at the warden, aka Mom. I stare at my ceiling, willing my heart rate to return to normal. I swipe a hand through my sweat-soaked hair across my forehead and let out a huff of breath. *Fuck.*

Sitting up on my elbows, my eyes scan my surroundings and stop on the outfit I have laid out for today. Savvy and I spent hours painstakingly choosing our back-to-school attire. I was so confident in my choice. Savs assured me it was hella hot in a very "Catholic schoolgirl" kind of way.

My eyes travel over the black cardigan, enveloping the satin, forest green tank top —the very tank top that makes the girls look ah-mazing. Down further to my favorite skirt. It's one that I've worn on days when I need the ego boost. Days where extra armor was necessary. I felt beautiful in that skirt.

As I take in the dark green and black plaid of my previously favorite garment, my stomach churns, and all I want to do is set the fucking thing on fire.

Welcome to senior year, Charlie.

Chapter 13

Fall 2005

I'm absentmindedly staring out of the passenger window as Mom, and I make our way to school when I feel a hard pinch to the underside of my left arm.

"Ow, what the fu.." I start as I rub the sore spot.

"Oh, please finish that sentence, little girl. I will pull this car over and shove your ass in a snowbank."

Damn, Mom's sass level is off the charts this morning.

I glare back at her, rubbing the now sore spot, "Why did you pinch me?"

"Because I asked you a question, and you were ignoring me," she replies haughtily.

I roll my eyes, but after my nightmare, I have no energy left to sass her back. "What did you ask?"

"I asked if you had anything specific planned for Thursday afternoon. I have an appointment, and I need a driver," she says. It takes my brain longer than normal to catch up.

"I don't have anything going on. I can go with you. Is everything okay?"

"I don't need you to go with me. I just need you to drop me off and pick me up after about three hours. I'll let you know a more direct time after I confirm with the office." she reaches over and pats my thigh, her attempt at reassurance, I guess. "They are just doing a routine procedure that requires a light sedation, and I can't go to the appointment unless I have a confirmed driver."

"Okay, I can do that." I search her face, but she seems chill, so I let it go. For now.

* * *

I can't seem to shake the unease I've felt since my rude awakening this morning. I couldn't tell you one thing that's been said during my classes. Dazedly, I wander down the hallway to put my books in my locker and head to the cafeteria for lunch.

A warm hand wraps around my waist and jerks me to the side. I blink out of my reverie with a start and look at Jason's handsome but concerned face.

"Babe, you almost walked right past your locker. What's up?" he asks.

I shake my head to dispel the fog in my brain, and I offer him a weak smile. "Yeah, sorry about that. I didn't sleep great last night, and I'm paying for it today."

He doesn't look convinced, but I just want to forget about it and go to lunch. I wrap my arms around his neck and give him a full-lipped kiss before I pull away and grab his hand, leading him toward the cafeteria.

"So that's a thing again?" Jason asks, using our joined hands to point out my best friend, who's currently sitting on Adam's lap, talking to a few members of the cheer team as he rubs his large hand up and down her back. I can't help but laugh. "Seems that way. You know Savvy is a free spirit. She loves as hard as she hates. And currently, she loves to hate Adam."

Jason leads me over to a secluded alcove in the crowded lunchroom. Tugging my hand, he pulls me down onto his lap as he rests his forehead against my chest and lets out a deep sigh.

I run my fingers through his long hair. "Are you okay, babes?" I question.

"I need to tell you something, and you're not going to like it, but I don't have a choice."

"Okay... Well, that doesn't sound good. What's going on, Jason?"

"So, every year, my family and a few of their friends go on an end-of-season camping trip. We will go for a week. Sometimes we rent cabins... and sometimes we stay in the Bianchi's big RV..." his eyes dart around the room before squeezing shut.

No. I swallow and try to steady my voice. He slowly raises his head from my chest to look into my eyes.

"Bianchi's? As in Jade Bianchi? Like your ex-girlfriend? You're going camping for a week with Jade."

"Not *with* Jade, her family is one of several that will be there, Sweets,"

"Okay, and in these several other families, how many have your ex-girlfriends in them?" I can't keep the bite out of my voice; I'm trying to be calm, but what the ever-loving fuck. How am I supposed to be okay with this?

"Charlotte, I get it, okay? I'm not happy about it either. I tried to get out of going, but my parents wouldn't budge. When that didn't work, I even asked if you could come along,"

"Let me guess, that was a big fuck no from your dad," I roll my eyes.

"I'm sorry, baby. I have to go." Jason says with exhaustion.

I scoff and roll my eyes, "Cool, yeah, fine. That's great. I hope you guys have a lovely time."

"Baby..." he pleads.

I stand abruptly, feeling the hot stinging at the back of my eyes. Logically, I know this isn't his fault. I also know that I trust him. It makes me uncomfortable, yes, but I need to believe that my boyfriend is a good man who will do the right thing.

It's that goddamn two-faced demon who I know just can't wait to rub this in my face. She wants him, she's made sure this was no secret, and I have a feeling she is going to use this time to try to sink her claws back into Jason.

"Look, I get it. You can't do anything about it, so it's fine, Jason. There's no point in continuing this conversation when it's a done deal."

I need to get out of here. I bend down and give him a light peck on the cheek, "Oh, silly me. I forgot, I told Jennifer I would meet her at her car before lunch was over to trade our Chemistry notes, so I'll catch up with you later." I don't give him time to respond as I turn and walk out the side door. He doesn't follow.

I wander through the parking lot. There are plenty of students taking their lunch hour outside. The weather is still nice and warm, even though it's a bit cloudy.

There's a trail used for cross-country skiing in the winter that goes through the woods surrounding the school. It goes for miles and is usually pretty empty during school hours. I start walking down the path, and even though I try to keep them in, the tears begin to fall.

I've been walking for about five minutes when the smell of cigarette smoke hits me as I approach a curve on the path. Turning the corner, a pair of black skate shoes catch my attention. My gaze travels upwards to his black jeans with a large hole in the right knee, topped with a deep gray hoodie and a black tightly fitted tee shirt with a few burn marks throughout.

Fuck me. Of course, someone would be witness to my meltdown. I quickly try to wipe my tears away when my hand suddenly stops moving. My wrist is being held gently away from my face by this complete stranger.

His eyes are hard. He must be pissed that I caught him smoking on school grounds. I won't tell on him, I don't care what he does out here, it's his business.

I open my mouth to tell him so when he yanks me forward, and I crash into his chest.

My heart is pounding so hard I can't hear anything. My vision is blurry with tears. My body is paralyzed in fear. My mouth won't work to scream for help. I'm powerless.

He's holding me so tight, but he's not doing anything else. I can feel his heartbeat against my cheek. It's steady and strong. How can he be so calm? I feel lightheaded. My breathing is erratic. I feel like I might pass out or maybe die.

Definitely die.

My knees are wobbly, and if this strong stranger wasn't holding me up, I have no doubt that I would've fallen to the ground by now. Why won't my fucking mouth work? Or my useless body? Scream. Push him away. Run. Get to safety.

Or... just let go. Stop everything. Stop fighting. Stop thinking.

Stop... breathing.

"Listen to my heartbeat, Little Bit. Breathe with me. Take a deep breath when I do." his strong hands stroke my back softly.

"You're okay. I've got you. Just breathe. Relax your body."

Thump, thump.

Thump, thump.

Thump, thump.

Yep, definitely going to die.

Chapter 14

"You feel that, Little Bit?" he asks softly, in a deep voice with a definite southern twang, his warm breath reaching my ear.

I hear it before my body can feel it. The familiar pitter-patter of raindrops hitting the crisp leaves around us.

"Take a deep breath for me," I do. My nose tingles with the unfamiliar scent of this boy. He smells like clean laundry soap, citrusy deodorant, and a fresh wave of smoke. Now that mixture swirls in my body with one of my favorite scents in the world, fresh rain.

Usually, fresh rain reminds me of Jason. But right now, all I can do is smell and feel this man in front of me.

"That's a good girl," he says as he rubs my back softly.

As my breathing begins to even out, my mind starts to catch up to the situation. With a start, I try to pull back.

"Ah, ah, Little Bit. Just another minute," he holds on firm, but he's not hurting me. *Who is this guy?*

I close my eyes and relax into his body, and he continues rubbing my back slowly.

It brings me back to when I would get sick as a kid; it's something my mom would always do to comfort me. I would be miserable on the couch, and she would come over, have me lay on my tummy with my head on her lap, and with one hand, she would rub gentle circles on my back, and with the other hand, she would stroke my hair.

When I feel one of his hands reach up and begin to run his fingers through my hair, I break. Hard sobs start to rack my body.

"That's right, darlin', let it out; I've got you."

I cry uncontrollably into his chest as my hands fist his shirt at his sides. His breathing stays steady, his heartbeat strong. I focus on the sound. Taking as deep of a breath as my lungs will allow, the calm starts to flow through me.

The stranger's hands come to my jawline. With a press of his thumbs, he gently tilts my face up to look at him, but I can't open my eyes. I'm so embarrassed. I just ugly cried all over this random person.

"Open your eyes, Little Bit," he coos.

I shake my head from side to side, squeezing my eyes tighter. He laughs softly and wipes my tears with his thumbs while still holding my face toward his.

"Please open your eyes,"

I let out a huff of breath as I open my eyes to land on my savior's face for the first time. His bright emerald eyes search mine out, and he smiles gently.

"There she is."

The stranger is traditionally handsome. He has short, dirty blond hair with gelled tips like most of the boys in school. Clean-shaven face with a sharp, square jawline and —unnatural to Alaska— tan skin. I don't recognize him.

Searching his eyes, I tilt my head to the side, "Who *are* you?" I question, my throat scratchy and hoarse from all the crying.

"I'm the psycho who's gonna drag you off the path, deep into them there woods, and have my wicked way with you," he whispers.

My whole body stiffens, and my eyes widen in fear, before I have too much time to dwell on my impending demise he laughs and loosens his hold on me, his hands falling gently to my lower back.

"I'm just messin' with you, Little Bit." his shoulders shake with humor, "Name's Zach Morris. Yes, like the TV show. I just moved to River View, and today is my first day."

"Why do you keep calling me that?" seems like a weird name, especially for someone you don't know.

He shrugs his large shoulders. "When I first saw you come around the corner, you had this faraway look on your face. You looked so lost and innocent. Also, you were sniffin' so much that your cute little nose just kept on bouncing up and down, kind of like a little bunny rabbit."

And then, he booped my fucking nose. I couldn't help but smile.

He abruptly let go of me and stumbled back, clutching his chest, "Oh good Lord, she smiles. And what a great smile it is." he points right at my mouth, "That, sweet girl, is all that should ever be seen on that beautiful face."

Blushing, I turn my face towards my feet and twist my hands together in front of me. His feet come into my line of sight, and he puts a finger gently under my chin, turning my face upwards. My hair covers my right eye, he takes his left pinky to ever so gently move the strands out of my eyes, giving him an unobstructed view of my face.

"Don't hide from me, Little Bit," he whispers.

"I have a boyfriend!" I shout suddenly, a little too loudly, right in his face.

This doesn't seem to faze Zach at all. He smiles down at

me. Maybe he didn't hear me, although I don't know how he couldn't with my loud, inappropriate outburst.

He chuckles, "I have no doubt about that. But I didn't ask... and I don't care."

"Come, sit with me," he says as he tugs my arm softly towards the log that his backpack is leaning against. I go with him and stare down at the now-wet chunk of wood. Before I can even speak a word, Zach removes his hoodie and places it on the log, and gestures to me to sit.

"Thank you," I say, my voice small. At least the rain has stopped now.

He sits beside me, his leg pressed right up against mine. No room for the Holy Spirit in between us.

That is a fun little saying my mom used to tease me about boys. *"Never let the little devils get too much in your personal bubble, Lola. Make sure to always leave room for the Holy Spirit."*

"It's possible I'll continue to call you Little Bit no matter what, but what is your actual name? Is it Kelly by chance?" he asks jokingly while bumping my knee with his.

"Ha ha," I reply dryly.

I clear my throat. I've embarrassed myself enough today. Squaring my shoulders, armor back in place, I smirk at his flirty question, and I thrust my hand towards him confidently, "I've always been an AC Slater fan myself. Charlotte Belle Johnson. You can call me Charlotte or Charlie. Most people do."

"Oh, Little Bit, I ain't most people." he grips my hand firmly and slowly shakes it while giving me what I'm sure is a panty-dropping smile for most girls. I'm not really sure how to respond to that. I appreciate his comfort and kindness, but boundaries are needed.

I have a boyfriend. I let go of his hand and, not too subtly, scoot away a little.

His grin falls a little at the new space between us. I have a feeling he uses his smiles and flirtatious personality as a mask, too.

Chapter 15

We sit in companionable silence for a few minutes. Both staring off into the trees. I feel very comfortable with Zach. That can't be a good thing, right?

Jason should be my only form of non-familial male comfort. But I find myself curious about this man.

"Why did you do that for me?" I finally break the silence.

Zach blows out a deep breath and picks up a leaf, and begins picking pieces of it off. "I could feed you a line about wantin' to wrap my arms around a pretty girl and be her knight in shinin' armor, but can I be real with you, Little Bit?"

I nod my head emphatically, "You can, I promise."

He looks down at the leaf; he's silent for a moment, "I recognized your pain. I don't know what happened, and if you wanna talk about it, I'm happy to listen, but in that moment, I knew you needed groundin'."

"Grounding? What do you mean?" I ask.

"It's a technique that helps with panic attacks. Have you had one before?"

"Is that what was happening?" I question.

"It can be different for different people, but a lot of times you can experience a racin' heart, have a hard time breathin', thoughts go catawampus, you can be overwhelmed by noises or groups of people, sometimes you feel locked or trapped in your body and you can't move your limbs or make words come out,"

Oh my God, many of those things have happened to me, especially lately. I had no idea. I suddenly feel very vulnerable. I lean forward and wrap my arms around my knees, and rest my chin on my thighs. The tears start welling up again.

"Hey, there's nothin' wrong with you, sweetheart. Panic or anxiety attacks are not your fault, and once you learn to recognize some of the warnin' signs, you can put some steps in place to help ground yourself,"

"Like what?"

"Somethin' you can try is the three-three-three rule." he holds up three fingers and begins to tick them off, "Name three things you can see, three things you hear, and move three parts of your body."

He looks down at the ground, moving loose rocks with his shoe before he continues, "What I did was provide you a groundin' touch. Think of it like a swaddle for babies. With you pressed against my chest, you could focus on the sound of my heartbeat and stop all the noise in your brain. I said soothin' words and held you until you felt more in control."

I laugh, a little uncomfortable with the seriousness of the conversation, so I try to deflect with humor, "What would you know about babies?"

"Oh, I have three of my own—triplets," he states matter-of-factly.

Oh shit. My mouth is suddenly very dry, "A-are you serious?" I stutter out.

He stares at me with a dumbfounded look on his face, like I am the crazy one for questioning this high school boy's parental status.

He finally breaks eye contact and starts snickering. Of course, he's not serious. A surge of relief goes through my body.

"So, how did you know to do all that…" I wave my hand to the area we were standing in before when he was calming me down.

A sad look washes over his face, and he turns away from me. We sit in silence for what seems like forever before he clears his throat.

"My dad is in the military. He was deployed immediately to Iraq after 9/11. He spent a full two years there with no R&R," he pauses for a moment, staring off into a memory, "When he came back…things were different. He would get madder than a hornet over nothin', got confused a lot, and startled easily. My house became Hell. He would scream at my mama and me. He would throw things against the wall when he couldn't get the words out. Mama finally gave him a choice: go to counselin' or lose his family. We had a few family sessions and were given some 'tools' to help when he was in that state."

"Oh my God. I'm so sorry. I can't imagine going through that. It must've been terrifying." I want to comfort him; I can't imagine feeling unsafe in my own home.

"I've never told anyone about this, Little Bit. I have no fuckin' idea why I just told you."

"Zach, I know you don't know me from Adam, but you can trust me. I would never betray your secrets. You can tell me anything." I try to give him my most trustworthy expression.

"I can, can't I? You really mean that." It's not a question.

He reaches over and gently moves his knuckles along my bicep, sending goosebumps through my body.

"You just have a way about you. I wanna tell you things and

let you know things about me. I think you and I are gonna be great together,"

"Great *friends* together," I correct with a smirk.

"Sure," he laughs like he's in on a joke I don't know.

As we continue to sit in companionable silence, I find myself daydreaming about sitting in my favorite spot at Sky Ridge.

The weather is perfect. There are very few clouds in the sky. The sun is high and illuminating my beautiful hometown. I can feel the light breeze across my face, whirling through my loose hair. I close my eyes and take a deep breath. An elbow softly touches mine on top of the picnic table, and as I look over, my gaze locks with emerald green ones. Eyes that definitely don't belong to my boyfriend.

Friends, Charlotte. *Just. Friends.*

Chapter 16

I shouldn't be avoiding Jason the way I have been. He's reached out several times, and I haven't flat-out ignored him, but I have been very short and direct in answering. I know it's not his fault, but I hate feeling this way. I'm not normally such a territorial person. I don't chase boys. I have avoided relationships purely because I don't like the drama that tends to go with them.

It's never seemed worth it before. But no boys have been Jason. I know I love him. I want to tell him, and I had been preparing to, but now it just seems wrong. How can I tell him that I'm in love with him when our relationship is rocky? I don't want him to feel like I'm trying to manipulate the situation. I also don't want to pretend I'm okay with something that makes me uncomfortable.

Do I trust him? I thought I did. Would I have this bad gut feeling about the two of them being together for a week and sleeping in the same place if I truly trusted him? Ugh, I hate this. If Jade hadn't been such a twat about things and actively trying to steal my boyfriend, I think I'd be able to move past my jealousy. But after the shit she's pulled? Fucking. Hell. No. I don't want her anywhere near Jason. Why isn't he fighting harder against it?

* * *

"Lola, are you ready to go?" My mom shouts from the front of the house. I had totally spaced that I needed to take her to her procedure today.

"Yep, coming!" I grab my favorite hoodie off the back of my bedroom door and give myself a little spritz of perfume before heading to meet her.

We make idle chat on the way to the medical plaza; when we get closer, I ask, "Do you want me to come in and wait with you?"

"No, you don't need to do that. Just be back here by 4:30 pm to pick me up. Just so you're prepared, they have to bring me out in a wheelchair. It's just their policy when you've been under sedation,"

"Aren't people really talkative when they have anesthesia? Like say all kinds of random stuff and always tell the truth? I can ask you anything I want to know, and you have no choice but to be honest. Maybe I can ask for that new car!" I tease her, but I don't miss the slight look of concern that briefly passes over her face before she pastes on a smile.

"Anything I say under the influence isn't admissible in a court of law. I can't make any legally binding decisions either, so..." she sticks her tongue out at me like a child.

I pout at her. "Fine then, be that way," she pats my knee, and I think I see a little glassiness over her eyes before she reaches for the door handle. She gets out and closes the door. Before I pull away, I see her at the entrance, she takes a large breath in and out and then looks back at me, blows me a kiss, squares her shoulders and enters the building.

* * *

I walk into the Coffee Hut with my face buried in my phone. My brain is on overdrive, trying to figure out how to respond to Jason's latest text.

Jason: I know ur upset, but there's literally nothing I can do. R U seriously going to punish me for not having a choice? What the fuck do U want me to do, Charlotte?

Charlotte. Not Sweets.

I start typing and delete my words over and over. I don't know what to say to that. Now *he's* mad that *I'm* mad? Jason has never spoken to me this way. I don't even know what to say. I don't want to make things worse. I just need some time to think.

I am about to put my phone away when I collide with a body in front of me.

"Oh shit, I'm sor.." I don't get the words out because another guy I don't have the right words for is standing before me. *Fuck.*

"Charlotte, good to see you didn't get mauled by a bear or run down by a plow truck or perish in an earthquake or one of the many other gruesome ideas that came to mind when you completely disappeared and never returned my texts or calls." a very angry Dean says.

He's not wrong to be pissed, I for sure took the cowards way out. I did not show up for our coffee date, and when he reached out, I ghosted. I wasn't sure how things would go with Jason. It wasn't my intention to hurt Dean. I was being selfish and didn't want to face him since I chose another boy over him.

As much as I am not mentally in a place to talk with my ex right now, I know it's the right thing to do.

I sigh, defeated. "Dean, can we talk?" I gesture to an empty couch at the backside of the room. I don't need an audience for yet another humiliation.

He laughs, and it sounds anything but humorous, "Sure, I'd love to, Charlotte. After you," he holds an arm out in front, gesturing to me to walk first. I can feel the anger rolling off him in waves. I make my way to the oversized plush loveseat and sit with my right foot under me, turned slightly towards the middle. Dean takes the seat beside me.

Gathering as much courage as I can, I start from the best place I can think of,

"I'm so sorry. For several things. I shouldn't have ignored your messages and calls. I owe you an explanation."

"I'm not sure I give a fuck what your reason is. I clearly don't mean shit to you. That's all I really need to know." as he turns to walk away, I gently grab his wrist. He freezes in place and looks down at me with confusion and a lot of contempt.

"Please, Dean. Please just give me five minutes of your time, and then you will never have to speak to me again if that's what you want."

He chews on his lip in thought. I found that sexy once upon a time; now, it just makes me nervous. He blows out a deep breath and looks toward the ceiling before slowly sitting back down and turning toward me, "Fine, you have five minutes. Not a second more. I'm done wasting my time on you."

Ouch, that hurt. Not that I want him to invest any more of his time in me, but just the callous way he said it, I did this. Made him hate me. He's hurting, and it's my fault. But this isn't about me. This is about doing right by him.

There's no easy way to bring this up. Dean doesn't go to RHS, so he doesn't know Jason, and he doesn't have many friends at my school that I know of.

"So, you remember when we last hung out at the movies with Stacy?" Of course, he remembers when he joined his sister and me for a movie night. That was the night Chad went apeshit, and Dean hauled ass out of there with Stacy to avoid getting jumped by Chad and his buddies while I stormed off and met his replacement.

"Mhm," he responds dryly

"Well, that night, I was really upset at what happened. I had just punched Chad in the face for knocking me down and trying to hurt you, and I was storming away when someone started chasing after me,"

Dean's face pales, maybe I didn't phrase that correctly. He probably thinks something bad happened to me because he left me there.

I shake my head profusely, "Nothing bad happened, I swear," he visibly relaxes, so I continue, "It was a boy I had never met before; he wanted to make sure I was okay. I don't know Dean. I'm not sure how to describe it, but when our eyes met, it just felt right. Like two puzzle pieces clicking toge..,"

"Charlotte, can you spare me the sappy fucking details of this story and get to the point."

He's angry. I can't fault him for that. I take a deep breath and shove my sarcastic bitchy remark way, way, *way* deep down.

"You're right, I'm sorry. The point is, I met someone. The day that I was supposed to meet you here," I gesture around the room, "he asked me to be his girlfriend."

Dean scoffs, and I see him squeezing his hands in fists on his thighs. I know this is hard to hear.

Honestly, I know that Savvy was right that Dean and I were never really good together. We were convenient. We were comfortable. He's always been more invested in us than I ever was.

But like everyone else in my life, he's attracted to the idea of me. The version of me that I show the world. Not the real me.

And that's not his fault. He has no idea that he never had all of me.

Chapter 17

I close my eyes and will the courage to burst forth and finish this conversation.

"I just want to be honest with you, Dean. We've known each other for a long time, and I want to do right by you, even if it's long overdue." he cocks an eyebrow and purses his lips together, but he lets me continue.

"The details aren't important unless you feel like you need them. I want to tell you that I am truly sorry for my lack of communication. That wasn't right, and you deserve so much more than that. I take full responsibility, and I understand if you hate me and think I'm a piece of shit." I try so hard to keep the quake out of my voice; it's taking everything I have to hold back the tears.

Dean's face softens, and he reaches a hand over to squeeze my lower thigh. I look down towards my lap and squeeze my eyes shut so tightly that I see a lightning bolt from behind my lids. The first tear falls.

"Hey. Look at me, Charlie," *Back to Charlie*, he can't hate me if he's calling me Charlie, right? I slowly raise my head and meet his eyes. He has a light, easy, lop-sided smile on his face.

"Am I mad? A little. Do I hate you? Not at all. I wish I could sometimes. It would make things easier. Do I think you're a piece of shit? Eh," he drags the H out and gives my thigh a squeeze again; there's nothing sexual about the touch; it's comforting.

His shoulders shake with restrained laughter; I playfully punch him in the shoulder, "Ugh, shut up, asshole."

His smile slowly fades to a more serious expression, "But for real, Charlie, I do forgive you. What you did was shitty, and if nothing else, I thought we were friends first. As your friend, you should've been honest with me. I'm not going to beat you up any more about it, it sure seems like you are doing a good job of that all on your own."

He's not wrong; this has been eating me up inside. I was just being too much of a chicken shit to address it. The universe has funny ways of forcing us into uncomfortable situations to right some wrongs.

I start to open my mouth to apologize again, and he holds his hand up, stopping me.

"Though it may seem crazy, I am actually happy for you. You look good. You seem content, and that's something that has been missing for a while. I know you think you have to hide yourself behind these walls you've built to keep everyone out, but you don't. I hope this guy deserves you and he treats you well. And I hope you let him in, Charlie," he gives me a knowing look.

I am full-on crying now, not sad tears, well, maybe a little bit sad. This is goodbye, to Dean and me, to whatever was or may have been. This chapter is officially closed, and for the first time since we've known each other, I think it's closed on his end.

I launch myself at him and wrap my arms around his neck. He wasn't ready for it, so he sinks backwards into the couch with a chuckle before squeezing me tightly with his giant arms.

"Thank you for being so amazing, Dean. You are going to make some lucky girl so happy someday. I want that for you. You are going to do great things with your life. I have no doubt about it. I love you, as a friend, and I always will." I whisper into his neck as we have our final embrace.

He pulls away first and puts his hand softly on my cheek, "I love you too, Charlie. Always. But I think it's best if we don't see each other for a while. I'm leaving for college in a few months, and I think a clean break will be best for me." I know he's right. I need to respect his wishes. So, I give him one final squeeze, *there's that damn lightning bolt again*, before pulling away and letting him go with a sad smile and a wave.

I sit back with a sigh, feeling lighter than I have in a while. I pull my phone back out to kill some time before I go get Mom. As I look around the room, I see a flash of long onyx hair as someone turns the corner outside the building.

* * *

As I pull up to the curb, I can't help but bust out laughing at the sight before me. Mom is currently giving the —much younger than her— male nurse what I'm sure she believes to be a seductive look, but her eyes are droopy, her hair is wild and sticking up in several directions, and her mouth is hanging open.

She looks like she spent the last three days hoochie-cooin' through bars.

I stroll up without a care in the world, "Hey, Momma, what cha doin'?"

She turns that droopy gaze in my direction and smiles so wide that a tiny dribble of drool slides down the side of her mouth. I bite the fuck out of my cheek to keep from cracking up. This is so funny, but I don't want to embarrass her any more than she is currently doing for herself.

"Lola!" she slurs out. "Come meet Derek. Derek has taken good care of me today. And I'm trying to convince him that I'll take *real* good care of him in return," she attempts a wink, but you know, droopiness. So it comes out like a blink when you're outside, and your eyelashes get stuck together because it's negative ten degrees, and you just took a shower.

Derek and I exchange pleasantries. His cheeks are flaming red from my mom's repeated advances. I throw him a sympathetic smile and reach for Mom's hand,

"Come on, Momma, let's get you home; Derek needs to get back to work." She stumbles a little while standing up from the wheelchair, but that doesn't stop her mouth, "I've got something he can work!" she cackles and elbows me in the ribs. I lose my battle of wills and bust out laughing. Sorry, Derek, you're on your own. My mom is funny as fuck.

"I'm sure he could work it real good, too," she reaches out for his arm, and he looks horrified.

"AND you're done, Ms. Johnson. Time to go," I say as I start pushing her into the open car door. No sooner than the car door shuts, and Derek high tails it back into the clinic. While Mom blows kisses at his retreating form.

She is my favorite.

Chapter 18

"Get the fuck out of this bed." Savvy whispers angrily in my ear through the blanket that I have firmly pulled over my head.

I've barely left my bed over the last few days.

I hold my phone up to my face in my dark blanket cave and illuminate the space as I stare at Jason and my last text exchange from the other day.

Jason: I know ur upset, but there's literally nothing I can do. R U seriously going to punish me for not having a choice? What the fuck do U want me to do, Charlotte?

Me: I'm not punishing you. I thought I was doing the right thing by telling my boyfriend when something made me uncomfortable. Looks like that's where I fucked up.

Jason: Y are U making this a bigger deal than it needs to be? Don't U trust me?

Me: I thought I did.

Jason: Uh wtf does that mean?

Me: ...

Jason: ??

Me: I don't know, Jason. I trust you. I don't trust her.

Jason: Jesus, Charlotte. I'm tired of talking about this. U need to find a way to deal with this. This is so fuckin stupid. Let me know when ur done with this tantrum.

I never responded back to that and he hasn't reached back out. I'll see him at school.

"I don't want to. Leave me alone to wallow in self-pity. Save yourself, Savs, this is a sinking ship right here." I say, muffled by the blanket draping over my face.

Not bothered in the slightest, she smacks me right in the forehead.

"Ow, what the hell!" I shout in outrage as I fling the blanket off my head and glare at my best friend. She has the audacity to smirk at me; this was her plan all along. Piss me off to get me to react.

"This is what's going to happen, Charls. You're going to get out of this gross bed, stick every one of your greasy body parts in a shower and put on this fucking cute skirt," she throws said skirt at my face, "put some crimps in your hair and slap some eyeliner on and then you and I are heading to the skate park."

Before I can even start to refuse, this bitch grabs me by the ankle and yanks with all her might to pull me off the bed, and I hit the floor hard.

"Fucking hell, Savannah! I think you broke my fucking ass!" I wince as I roll to the side to grab hold of my dresser to pull myself up. I stand in front of my full body mirror and lift my sleep shorts off the side of my ass, and sure enough, it's hella red and will most likely bruise. Fucking Savvy.

I glare at her as I grab the skirt she's now thrusting in my direction and head to the bathroom to get ready. As I look down at my bloody underwear, I swear under my breath. I should've known my rag was coming. I have been pretty emotional lately. I open the cabinet door to grab a tampon, only to find we don't have any.

What happened to the bulk box we had?

* * *

It's a little cooler today but still a decent late fall day, so we decided to walk to the skate park. Adam and his buddies like to hang out there, so I assume that's why she wants to go. Those two are so hot and cold, they need to make a choice and stick with it. I've told her this, over and over again.

But at this moment, with the current state of my own relationship, my advice means jack shit. I can't even seem to sort my own situation out. I'm not really sure how we got here. Jason and I don't fight. Why do I let Jade get under my skin so much?

If he wanted her, he'd be with her, right? Right. I'm being ridiculous. I need to tell him that I do trust him and I know he can't do anything about the camping trip. It is what it is, and he doesn't need me to make it worse. I don't want to keep having conversations over text, so tomorrow, I will tell him to his face, and we'll move past this.

With my mind at ease about that situation, I feel a bit lighter and add a pep to my step as we enter the park.

I'm laughing at a story Savvy's telling me about her unfortunate wardrobe malfunction at the grocery store when the edge of her already short skirt got caught on the metal of someone's shopping cart. They went one way, she went the other, and her skirt came apart. She accidentally flashed her ass cheeks to poor Mr. Seymore, a sweet eighty-something local.

Savvy being Savvy, just winked at the old man and popped her gum loudly, and feigned embarrassment. "Oh dear me, whatever shall I do about my backside being exposed to all the prying male eyes in the store," she even put the back of her hand dramatically against her forehead like she was about to faint.

I love my best friend, but her tall tales can get a little wild. But Savvy is just crazy enough that I'm never quite sure if something did or didn't happen. It's entertaining nonetheless, so I have fun with it and with her.

"No fucking way, what did he do?" I gasp.

"He looked terrified of all this fine young flesh. He used his shaky hands to pull off his jacket and held it out to me as far as he could so we didn't have to actually touch,"

Now I know my bestie, and there's no way she let him get away with the distance.

"So I made sure to caress his hand in a very soft and gentle way when I took the jacket. I leaned close and offered him my thanks in a breathy way." There it is.

"You are terrible. Leave that poor old man alone. You could've given him a heart attack."

That's just what this little town needs is a sweet old man dropping dead in the store and Savannah Mitchell's ass on display for all to see.

"At least he would've gone out with a good mental image," she laughs.

"You are a Godless Jezebel, Savs." I mock admonishment at her. She shrugs it off, and before she can offer me another inappropriate comment about Mr. Seymore, her gaze locks on something over my shoulder, and she stands there with her mouth hanging open.

"When's my birthday again, Charls?"

Um, that's a weird question to ask me.

"It's December twenty-second... why?" I question suspiciously.

"Cause', I know what I want." I can almost see the drool

appearing on her chin.

"Okay, I'll bite. What do you want for your birthday?" I nudge her arm playfully.

She lifts her arm and points at where she's been looking. I turn my head to see what she's pointing at. The sun is blocking my view, so I lift my hand to cover the top of my eyes.

My eyesight clears, and I get a flash of a very shirtless, tan, sweaty boy wearing a backward ball cap atop his dirty blond hair and sunglasses on his face.

"Him," she says simply.

I roll my eyes; this girl is so boy-crazy. Good luck to her newest victim; he's going to need it. She links arms with me, walking us closer to the unknown guy who is now skating in the opposite direction, so we are staring at his back. His very toned and muscular back.

Savvy starts primping herself. I've always envied her self-confidence. When she wants something, she goes for it. No hesitation, she just puts herself out there. And guys? They are drawn to her like a moth to a flame. I get it; her self-confidence is attractive.

I sit on the edge of the skating bowl with my bare legs dangling downwards as I watch my best friend strut her best stuff toward the mysterious, hot dude.

There are many grunts and loud thuds, booms, and slams as the boys around me exert themselves, trying different tricks on the obstacles in the park. A young boy, maybe ten or eleven, catches my attention. He is desperately trying to perfect an Ollie by snapping the tail of the board off the ground and bringing the entire board up into the air.

He keeps dropping his board. I silently give him encouragement to keep going. He'll get it. He looks in my direction, and his cheeks flame. He's embarrassed to mess up, especially in front of a girl. I give him a sincere smile and a thumbs up. He smiles brightly and gives it another go. He almost had it this time.

I keep watching him try, and when he lands it perfectly, I jump to my feet, clapping and cup my mouth to cheer loudly for him. He smiles so big and puffs his chest out as he starts heading towards his friends. No doubt to brag. I feel good for him; he deserves it.

I look around for Savs, and my breath flees my body. The beautiful, tan, shirtless specimen she's flirting with is staring directly at me, and those lush, verdant eyes pierce right through my skin.

Zach.

Chapter 19

I'm frozen in place. My thoughts are all over the place. I suddenly feel very aware of my surroundings.

Zach's attention is back on Savvy, but he briefly peers over at me every few seconds. I'm still standing here like an idiot. Why am I making this weird? *Just go over there and join their conversation. Go Charlotte. Move your feet. Go.*

"Hey, Charlie, who's the asshole flirting with my girl?" Adam flicks his sweaty hair out of his face like a dog. I make a disgusted noise when I feel wetness hit my leg. Gross.

"Don't start, Adam. You and I both know Savvy belongs to no one," I lightly punch him in the arm. Damn, his bicep is hard; when did he get so built?

He gives me a mischievous grin, and I know I'm fucked. Before I can get words out or sprint away to safety, Adam lunges towards me and leans down to throw my body over his shoulder. He lifts me like I weigh nothing.

I let out probably the most unladylike screech ever. He's laughing and grabs his board, and we start to move. This motherfucker is going to try to balance me and skate at the same time. Fuck no.

"Put me down, you prick! You drop me, and you are so dead!" We've drawn the eyes of most of the skate park patrons at this point.

Adam just laughs and claps his big hand on my ass. Oh shit. I feel *way* too much breeze right now. Fuck my fucking life. I'm wearing a goddamn skirt, with very light pink, cheeky panties. Panties that are currently on display for all to see.

Hoots, hollers, and whistles fill the air as we glide around.

I could flip out. Bang my fists on his back. Scream obscenities at him. Make threats. But I don't do any of that.

When I press myself up off his back a little to look around, I see my best friend with a not-at-all shocked look on her face; she's used to Adam's antics. She seems amused by the situation. The green-eyed boy beside her, though? He looks murderous.

And for some reason, that thrills me.

Savvy starts heading in our direction with Zach hot on her heels.

"Put my best friend down, you fucking caveman," Savs says through a smile.

There's no jealousy in her tone. She knows Adam and I are as platonic as two people can get. He is like my brother from another mother. Also, since I briefly dated his brother, aka "Chad the Douche", that is a one hundred percent no-fly zone for me.

"Nah, I don't think I will. She's the perfect addition to make my workout a little more challenging," he does a little pop-up of his board, and I grip his t-shirt with all my might. It is very possible that he will drop me by accident.

Adam's doing small circles around Savs and Zach, showing off.

"Who's this dude, Savs?" Adam asks, trying and failing, to keep the animosity out of his voice.

I start to relax again when suddenly, we are airborne. I shut my eyes tight to brace myself for impact. When that doesn't happen, I open my eyes, confused.

I am being held by the fabric of my shirt from behind, my hair dangling forward in my face. Strong arms wrap around my waist to straighten me back to a standing position.

"Why am I always savin' you, Little Bit?" a deep voice breathes into my ear from behind. It sends shivers throughout my whole body. My heart is pounding at an unnatural pace. I'm not sure if it's from my almost disastrous wipeout or the boy who saved me from it.

"Fuck. Charlie, are you okay? There was a fucking rock that got stuck in my wheel. I am so sorry. Are you hurt?" gone is the humorous, carefree expression. This is the serious and concerned Adam.

My gaze flicks up to Savvy's, and I see a curious look on her face as her eyes are glued to my mid-section, where I instantly remember Zach has his arms wrapped around me. He has yet to let go, and I also haven't pulled away.

That shocks me into action, and I spring away from Zach like my ass just caught fire and dust myself off from the imaginary debris.

Savs narrows her eyes at my reaction, her stare bouncing back and forth between him and me. She tilts her head to the side, "Do you two know each other?" *Motherfucker*. I never told her about what happened in the woods that day. I didn't tell anyone.

I would like to believe I didn't say anything because I'm embarrassed that I had a total meltdown. But I don't think that's it. If I force myself to examine it closer, I know why I didn't tell anyone. That was just for us. Zach and me. We each shared a piece of ourselves with a total stranger in those woods.

At that moment, I felt closer to him than I have to anyone in my life. Ever. Including my best friend and boyfriend. And that terrifies me.

I wanted to keep that interaction safe and hidden from the outside world. It was pure and raw. I don't want reality to taint it.

It's not that I didn't think I'd ever see him again, but I just didn't think he'd really acknowledge me.

Whenever I imagined our next meeting —*yes, I've imagined it*— he was always charming and larger than life. He would give everyone around him the same smile, the same laugh, the same attention that he gave me. Just like a *friend* would.

I turn back to look at him, and his eyes are searching mine for how to handle this. Like he knows I want to keep that interaction just between us and he's willing to go along with whatever I say. I choose two things in this moment; to protect our woods experience and keep that just for us and to tell a version of the truth.

I nod my head at her question, "Yes, we met briefly last week at school," I see him nodding his agreement as well. "He helped me with a problem I was having in class."

Savs made a slow nod of her head. I can tell she wants to ask more questions, but I decide to thrust her back into the spotlight,

"Have you two properly met?" I question, Savannah smiles brightly as I push her back to get her into Zach's airspace, happy to be the focus again and shakes her head.

"Savvy, this is Zach," I hold my hand in his direction. "Zach, this is my best friend Savannah. Everyone calls her Savvy." He pastes that charming smile back on and holds his hand out for hers, "Ma'am,"

She giggles, *fucking giggles*, as she takes his hand in hers and holds the shake for longer than I'd like.

I don't know how I know, but I know for a fact that the smile he's using isn't real. She's getting a fake version of Zach.

And for some reason, that makes me feel a little better.

Chapter 20

I feel like Ride of The Valkyries should be playing as I enter school. I'm filled with an overwhelming sense of dread as I make my way down the hallway towards my locker. I haven't spoken to Jason since our texts, and I never responded to his last one.

I wore a comfy, gray, cropped knitted sweater today and some high-waisted light-wash jeans, and currently, I feel like my skin is crawling. This is usually my go-to comfort outfit, but I'm so on edge that it feels like wool wrapped in fiberglass particles and dipped in honey.

My heart is beating in my throat, and my palms are getting sweaty; I rub them on my jeans.

I smell him before I see him. I close my eyes and take a deep breath before turning around. He doesn't look angry; he doesn't have much of an expression at all.

"Hi," I sound meek even to my own ears, and instantly, I hate it. I'm not this girl.

I clear my throat and try again, "I wanted to apologize for last week and really most of our conversations lately."

I'm proud of how steady and confident my voice sounds when really, I feel like I could crumble at any moment.

"Me too, Sweets. I'm already frustrated with everything

going on, and I've tried talking to my parents, but they won't budge. I want to make you happy and comfortable." he pauses to take my hand and swipe a tendril of hair off of my eyes. "But you have to understand that Jade is not just my ex; she's my friend, too." I nod my head along.

I already know all this. Though I hate Jade's stupid, beautiful face, and part of me hopes she walks face-first into a spider web and then falls into a large, decrepit pile of fish guts, I need to give him trust and respect.

This isn't about me and Jade or even Jason and Jade. This is *our* relationship; she has no part in it, and I need to stop giving her power over me.

"I understand. I'm not going to lie and say I'm over my issues with it, *but* I do trust you, and I'm done bringing it up. Can we just move on?" I ask earnestly.

He reaches out and pulls me by my hips closer to him and places his forehead against mine, his lips just a hair's breadth away, "I'd love to, baby. And I'm sorry, too. I let my anger get the better of me and took it out on you, and that wasn't right. I apologize for that." he wraps me snugly in his arms and presses a firm kiss to my lips.

When he tries to pull away sooner than I'm ready for, I pull his face back into mine and kiss him back with even more vigor.

We stand in the hallway staring at each other with goofy smiles on our faces. Every part of me is screaming to tell him, 'I love you', but it's not the right time. Soon.

* * *

By the time lunch rolls around, I rush to the cafeteria. Now that things are okay between Jason and me, my appetite is back in full force.

Standing in line waiting for my turn to pick what I want to eat today, I do a little hungry happy dance by shimmying my shoulders and bopping my head from side to side. I hear a deep chuckle from behind me.

I turn to find Zach watching me in amusement. His eyes lit with laughter, and his smile soft and genuine. I flash him a big grin.

"It's taco day, Zach! Everyone should be dancing in this line right now. RHS tacos are the literal best!" I hip-check him, and he just shakes his head and laughs.

He waggles his brows and hip-checks me back, "Is that so? I'm not so sure I believe you about that." he lowers his voice and conspiratorially whispers, "But I'd love to try some of *your* taco,"

I scoff. Clearly, Zach doesn't know me very well. *Everyone* knows I don't share food. I am weirdly possessive over my meals. I also have a weird thing about sharing milk. Water, soda, juice, or coffee don't bother me. But if someone gets near a milk product of mine, I absolutely won't touch it again. *Gag.*

I growl at him, "Get your own damn taco, pretty boy!"

I get right in his face and poke my finger into his chest to punctuate my words, "I do *not* share food." I fold my arms across my chest, feeling smug, and give him a haughty look.

His next words wipe that shit straight off my face.

He leans in close, swipes his tongue across his bottom lip, boops my fucking nose again, and whispers, "Oh Little Bit, I wasn't talkin' about the food."

I... he... *what*?!

"Next!"

He smiles widely at me before spinning me around and gently shoving me to the counter to order my food.

"What'll it be, doll?" The gravelly low voice of our beloved elderly lunch lady croons at me.

"Um, yes, I'll take one tac.." I don't even get through the request before a voice slices through the crowd.

"Charls! I want one, too!" Savvy shouts from way too far away, drawing the attention of most of the lunchroom. She gets some dirty looks from a few of our classmates but most just ignore her. They are used to the outgoing personality of my bestie.

"Make that two tacos with extra cheese, please, Doris." I love this old lady; she is so sweet, and high school kids are assholes. They always treat her like she doesn't matter, but that never stops her from being incredibly kind.

"New boyfriend, doll?" Doris leans around me to peek up at Zach, who's grinning like the cat who got the cream.

The way Doris' eyes light up, it's clear she would approve if this were indeed the case.

I snort, "N..." Before I can get the full two-letter word out, the charmer himself steps forward with his hand outstretched to Doris.

"Ma'am," he tips his invisible hat. I roll my eyes. "Name's Zachariah Morris, a pleasure to meet you. Unfortunately, I have yet to convince this beautiful girl to accept my affections. So I've firmly placed myself in the role of her new best friend." he winks at me.

I can't help myself. I'm starting to laugh now. His southern accent is so strong right now, straight out of an old western. But Doris is eating this shit up like he just wrote and performed an award-winning sonnet.

She puts her hand over her heart and sighs, "Sweetheart, they don't make 'em like this anymore. If I were you, I'd snatch him up. Hell, if I was twenty years younger,"

I choke on air with a gasp, " Twenty years? How old *are* you, Doris?"

"Okay, maybe thirty years or so." she pats the top of my hand and brings her finger to her mouth in a "Sh" motion before turning to grab my food.

"That'll be four dollars, Doll," Doris says as she slides the tray towards me, and as I go to reach out for it, Zach swats my hand away and lays a ten-dollar bill down for her. He picks up the tray for me with one hand, and with his other, he guides me gently out of line. I hear Doris softly chuckle as we walk away.

"You didn't have to pay for my food, Zach." Why would he even want to?

When he doesn't respond, I look over at him, and my eyes widen in horror as I watch him lift a taco to his lips. Granted he doesn't take a large bite, however, he takes a bite nonetheless. My mind stutters; I told him I don't share food. I can't give Savvy the partially eaten taco.

"Mm. Little Bit, I knew your taco would be mouth-wateringly delicious." he hands the tray back to me and turns to walk away, and winks, "Enjoy."

Leaving me staring after him trying to figure out what the fuck just happened.

And why it made me feel all warm and tingly inside.

Chapter 21

Fall 2005

I feel numb as I watch Jason pack his suitcase for the camping trip his family—and fucking Jade's— leaves for in the morning. I've occupied myself over the last few weeks by pretending this trip wasn't happening.

I tried to let it go and get over my insecurities about it. I really did. But alas, doubt has crept in over the last twenty-four hours. It's been like a fucking doomsday clock in my head.

I want to scream and cry and punch something, preferably Jade's stupid smug face.

On Friday, before lunch was over, she walked by our table and cleared her throat loudly. I looked up, and she just gave me a huge grin and winked at me. She never slowed her gait; all she wanted was to get my attention for the taunt.

Of course, no one but me saw this, so when I looked around at my friends and boyfriend for confirmation of what the fuck just happened, no one was the wiser as to what had occurred. Just great.

I've done what I was supposed to do. To everyone else's

knowledge, I've let it go, and I'm totally okay with my boyfriend's weeklong trip with his ex-girlfriend. But I'm not. I'm really fucking not.

I feel so out of control. Of everything. I had another panic attack last night, followed by the same nightmare of my bloodied, lifeless body on the ground. Just for funsies, though, this nightmare was accompanied by black and white polaroids of Jade and Jason all over the floor. In the pictures, the two of them were sweaty and tangled up in sheets on a bed.

I woke up and ran to the bathroom to throw up the entire contents of my stomach. I laid on the bathroom floor and stared catatonically at the ceiling for God knows how long. When I finally sat up and went to rinse my mouth out, I noticed blood on the sink handle.

I flipped my hand over and saw four bloody crescent shapes from where I clearly dug my fingernails into my palm. I never even felt it. I didn't sleep again after that.

"Sweets?" Jason asks softly,

I zoned out and missed what he said.

"Yeah, sorry. What did you say?" I offer him a sheepish smile.

"I asked if it would be okay with you if I took something of yours with me. So when I miss you because I will miss the hell out of you, I have something to remind me of you."

I stand and walk to his door and shut it gently. I turn to face him and lean against it, and I look him up and down. Taking in his ratty band tee and black basketball shorts down to his bare feet. Something about seeing him dressed down like this makes me imagine a future together.

We would have a large modernized log cabin on ten acres with Spruce, Pine, and Birch trees as far as the eye could see.

Two dogs, Alaskan Malamutes. Two kids, a boy and a girl, twins. A luxury SUV for me and a jacked-up truck for him. Matching snow machines and fishing gear.

Gage and Sophie, the twins, would wake us way too early on Christmas morning, and I would shoo them out of the room with promises to make some peppermint hot chocolate if they went and sat by the tree to start sorting gifts and wait for us to get there.

I would then give my husband—because, of course, Jason and I are married in this fantasy— a very merry Christmas morning present, naked.

"What's on your mind, Sweets?" Jason asks, bringing me back to the current moment.

I don't say anything, but I walk over to him and gently close his suitcase, and move it to the floor. Then I walk Jason to the bed and gently press him backward until he lays flat. I climb up to straddle him, his hands instantly finding my ass.

I lean down and kiss him, softly at first, a few pecks. He grinds his hips upwards to me, and I meet his pressure with equal fervor and movement of my hips.

He gently bites on my bottom lip, and when I gasp, he takes the opportunity to slide his tongue in and explore my mouth. As he licks and sucks, my hands lift up his shirt, seeking out any skin I can get my hands on.

He slides a hand forward to go in between my thighs, and he starts to rub me over my jeans.

I sit up and pull my tank top over my head, leaving me in just my black satin bra.

"This," he says while cupping my breast with his other hand.

"Huh?" I ask in confusion.

"This is what I want to take with me. Can I Sweets?"

I laugh, "I guess so. Won't you have to hide it so no one sees?"

His serious expression stops my laughter, he sits up while holding onto my back so I don't slide off him, and he looks me straight in the eyes. "I don't give a shit what anyone sees. If they have a problem with it, they can go fuck themselves."

I gulp and nod. What can I say to that? So I don't say anything. Putting my lips back to his, I slide my hands to my back and remove the bra for him.

As soon as my nipples hit the air, they pebble, and he groans. "Fuck, Sweets."

He flips me over onto my back, and we spend the next hour ravaging each other.

Little did I know, things would never be the same after this week.

Chapter 22

I haven't heard from Jason since Sunday. He warned me that, depending on the location of the campsite, there might not be cell reception but that he would try to contact me daily.

Well, I guess he's in a dead zone. Fantastic.

I have barely slept since my nightmare on Saturday night. When I do manage to fall asleep, I have some variation of the nightmare.

The only thing that seems to vary, though, is the pictures are now in color, and the color of the goddamn lingerie that Jade is wearing in the photos changes or what body part of Jason's she has her mouth on.

I can't breathe. I can't think about anything other than my boyfriend balls deep in another girl. The very thought of him with someone else twists my stomach violently. I can't be here anymore.

Though I usually can't use the car freely during the week, it's Thanksgiving break, and both Mom and I are home.

I walk into the living room and see her sitting on the couch reading. I know we don't have any plans until tonight, when my dad's flight comes in around midnight. My mom will go pick him up while I stay home and prep a few dishes to take over to Savvy's house tomorrow morning.

"Hey, Momma, can I borrow the car for a little bit?" I try to keep the shake out of my voice, but the instant look of concern she gives me tells me I was not very successful.

"Is everything okay, baby?" she asks.

I take a deep breath and wish for some calm to come over me. I know if I don't convince her that I'm okay, there's no way she'll let me leave or drive.

I offer her a weak smile, but it's the best I've got right now. "I'm good. I'm just missing Jason and was hoping to take my mind off it for a little while." I finally broke down and told her I was dating someone a few weeks ago.

I thought she'd be mad that I hid it from her for several months, but she just smiled and stared at me for a while. She squeezed my shoulders and said she was glad I was finding happiness. Then she drew me in for a long hug and cried.

The whole encounter was odd, but I was just relieved she wasn't upset that I didn't think about it much more after that. They haven't met yet, but she made me promise to introduce Jason to both her and my dad while he's in town, and I agreed. Now I just have to inform Jason.

"Okay, sweetheart. If you're sure, be back before dark please, the forecast is calling for snow." she holds out the keys for me and kisses the air in my direction before returning to her book.

I look like a freaking mess. I'm in a pair of Savvy's cheer sweats with the RHS logo down the sides and a threadbare sweater from my dad's Navy days.

My outsides definitely match my insides right now, and I couldn't give a fuck less.

I grab my favorite light blue fleece to throw on top and head out.

My thoughts are spinning wildly as I make the constant

twists and turns to get to the top of Sky Ridge. Passing all the large houses that line the road and disappear into private neighborhoods.

When I get to the parking lot, I shut the ignition off. There are no other sounds except the clicking of the engine cooling and my racing heart.

Thump, thump

Thump, thump

Thump, thump

I squeeze my eyes shut and press my palms into them. My breaths are coming in harsh pants. I feel like an icy dagger is slowly making its way through my chest and straight into my heart.

I rip my hands away from my face and slam them into the steering wheel, reveling in the sharp sting of pain that occurs with each force of contact. So I do it again.

Over and over.

A hot, burning sensation starts to creep up my legs; it feels like Hellfire licking at my skin. It continues its upward trajectory to my thighs, to my stomach, to my chest, to my neck, and finally to my head.

I have to dispel this toxic energy out of my body, or I may just fucking die—right here, right now.

I grip the steering wheel so tightly that I start to lose sensation in my fingertips, and I scream.

I scream as hard as my little body will allow. I scream for the pain. I scream for the heartache. I scream for the fear. I scream for the uncertainty.

I just fucking scream.

I scream until I run out of breath, and my throat feels like I've swallowed a dozen razor blades. A hot trail of tears streams uncontrollably down my cheeks; I don't bother wiping them away and ball my fists on my lap instead.

I stare straight forward, looking at everything and yet seeing nothing. My eyes rapidly dart from side to side, and darkness starts to creep into my vision.

I can't do this.

I can't feel like this anymore.

I don't *want* to feel like this anymore.

An eerie calm washes over me, and the fog begins to lift from my thoughts, determination setting in.

I *am* in control.

I read an article last year about this phenomenon that occurs when someone feels pulled towards danger.

Such as someone standing at the edge of a cliff and they get the sudden urge to jump. Or when driving at high speed, they get an impulsive need to jerk the wheel into oncoming traffic. Maybe while they dip their toes in the ocean, they get the sudden urge to just walk right into the calming waves and never come back.

You get the idea.

This phenomenon is known as l'appel du vide in French, translated into English as "The Call of the Void."

Our brains are designed to deal with this misinterpreted safety signal by encouraging us to move away from danger and not toward it.

The article stated that just because you experience "The Call of the Void" doesn't mean you have suicidal idealizations, and it's perfectly normal to encounter the fleeting feeling.

That's what it's supposed to be. Fleeting.

But what if that feeling doesn't go away?

What if I don't *want* it to go away?

Tap, tap, tap.

What if I turn this car back on?

Shift it in drive.

Grip the steering wheel tight with both hands.

Take my foot off the brake.

Press down on the accelerator as far as it will go.

Close my eyes.

And fly.

Tap, tap, tap.

I feel my lips lift into a smile as I envision flying off the cliff edge in front of me and laugh.

Thoughtless.

Painless.

Weightless.

Free.

Tap, tap, tap.

I loll my head towards the tapping noise on the window and latch on to the luminescent emerald green eyes staring at me, full of shock and worry.

And I laugh.

Chapter 23

Zach

I don't know what compelled me to follow the car into the parking lot. I was out for a run and saw it zoom by me when I was almost to the top.

I usually start at my house, which is about mid-way up Sky Ridge. I run all the way to the top, in a loop down to the bottom and back to the top again for a rest before heading back to my neighborhood. This gives me almost four miles daily.

I've had all this pent-up energy, and if I'm honest with myself, I've been lonely, so my only outlets are football, skating, and working out.

We done been in Alaska for a few weeks now, yet another place where I don't know anyone. No friends. No family nearby.

At least at my dad's previous duty stations, we were close to bigger cities, so I could at least explore and meet people and get my dick wet when the need arose.

What am I supposed to do in bum fuck nowhere?

I'm pretty sure the entire population of this state could've fit inside the Atlanta metro area.

Why couldn't he have figured out a way to stay for just the rest of the school year? Then I would've been off to college and on my own.

But no, like always, I don't get a fucking choice in my own life. His word is law, and I have just got to 'shut up, toe the line and deal with it'.

Because of our constant moving I don't have many people I would call actual friends, but I always have a whole lot of acquaintances around. Especially females. They're drawn to me and always have been. I guess I got that classic good ol' southern boy look.

I got the same sandy blond hair that my mama's got. It's a little longer on the top than on the sides. I keep it nice and gelled to give myself that windblown look the girls seem to love.

I'm fairly tall at 6'2. I take great pride in my body. In the off-season, I work out and skate all the time, so I'm lean but still muscular. My thighs could crush a full beer can.

I've been actively working on a six-pack, though I'm only sportin' a four-pack so far.

I hate being cooped up inside, so I maintain a naturally great tan on my skin from the hot Georgia sun.

My last hookup said I "had a totally lickable Adonis belt," whatever the hell that means. But she put her mouth on my pecker often, so she could say whatever she wanted about my body.

No shit, that chick could suck the chrome off a ball hitch.

Only second to my toned body is my uniquely green eyes—same eyes my old man has. The only good thing he ever gave me.

I reckon I'm pretty blessed in the looks department, and I

learned from an early age how to use that to my advantage.

A crooked smile, a wink, softly biting my lower lip, subtly flexing my arm muscles, running my fingers through my hair. Turning up the southern charm by throwing in a "ma'am, darlin', sweetheart, or honey".

The panties practically throw themselves at me.

If being a star footballer, toned physique, and charm aren't enough to make any female swoon, the fact that my family is from old money is guaranteed to seal the deal.

My Papaw and Mee-Maw have always spoiled me rotten. Probably to help make up for the fact that their son is an unfeeling bastard.

I've had one serious girlfriend, Dani. My dad and her mama were in the same unit and worked at three different bases together when we were younger before both being deployed to Iraq. Whenever I would start a new school, I always had her.

She was my first everything.

My first friend. My first kiss. My first handful of tiny jugs. My first addition to the spank bank. My first —and fucking thankfully only— premature ejaculation while fooling around. Most importantly, she was the very first warm slit I ever sank into.

She was my first and, most importantly, only love.

We talked about our lives together after graduation. We both wanted to go to the West Coast and attend UCLA.

Just two country bumpkins crashing into the big bad world together. I even asked Mee-Maw if we had a family heirloom-type ring for when I was ready to propose.

Everything changed right before junior year ended.

We had just got done knockin' boots at her house when we heard a noise. No one was supposed to be home. We skipped our last two classes so we could be here alone.

Her dad was visiting his sick mama in Tennessee, her mama was on duty for another few hours, and her little brother was at a friend's house until tomorrow.

We both rushed to get dressed, and I grabbed her little brother's aluminum baseball bat as we stalked down the hallway.

The noises continued to get louder and more intense. As we got closer, we could tell it was coming from her parents' bedroom.

We both looked at each other in confusion.

The confusion quickly went away when we started hearing moaning and grunting.

We both started busting a gut. Our hands flew to cover our mouths while we made our way back to her room.

Dani's parents were here, fucking in the daytime. Good for them.

Dani came to a stop in front of her bed. I walked behind her and wrapped my arms around her waist, and moved her hair off her shoulder so I could pepper it with kisses. When my lips touched her skin, I could feel her trembling.

So, I snuck my tongue out and licked a path from her shoulder to the pulsing point in her neck and sucked.

I could feel her intense rapid breathing through her stomach.

Something's wrong. "Baby, what's goin' on?"

She started shaking her head. "No, no, no. That ain't right."

"What ain't right, baby?" I gently turned her to face me, her face was ashen, and her baby blues were flooding with tears.

"Zee, my d-dad..."

I carefully steer her to sit on the bed and grab her hand, "What about him, darlin'?"

She stared intensely at me; she didn't speak for so long. I was afraid she might've forgotten how. Finally, she looked away to the bedroom door.

"H–he ain't here, remember?" What the fuck is she talking about? If her dad wasn't here, then... oh shit.

"Baby..." I tried to get her attention back on me, but she wasn't paying me no mind. Before I could get any other words out, she was on the move, and she wasn't fucking around.

I jumped up to go after her, and I arrived at the door she'd just flung open. She stood frozen in the hallway, catatonically staring at the scene before her.

I came to stand behind her and took in the events unfolding before our eyes.

I realized a few things. That definitely was not Dani's dad balls deep inside her mama on all fours. There ain't a snowball's chance in Hell for Dani and me now.

And my dad was a fucking dead man.

Chapter 24

Zach

That day changed everything. Dani told her dad. He flew back the next day and punched my old man in the face.

I laughed. My mama cried. Dani's mama apologized, not that anyone gave a shit.

My dad's enlistment was about over, and he had been discussing getting out entirely and having us plant roots here.

My mama told him he had two choices. To re-enlist and take the furthest duty station offered to him, or she would file for divorce and tell his chain of command that he was engaging in behavior unbecoming of an officer and fraternizing with his subordinate.

We found out the affair had been going on for more than a decade. Pieces of shit —both of them.

Dani's dad wouldn't even speak to his wife. He filed for divorce and took Dani to Tennessee. I haven't spoken to her since.

And obviously, my sperm donor chose door number one.

* * *

When I saw the car enter the parking lot of the lookout point, I watched it park and heard a gut-wrenching scream. My ass has never moved so fast. When I got to the door, my breath was ripped out of my chest when I saw the beautiful, tortured girl who was currently falling apart in front of me.

I bend down to her window and tap on it trying to get her attention. She's having a panic attack again.

She doesn't react.

I try the door handle, and it's locked.

I tap again. Her screaming has stopped, but I don't like the look on her face. It's like she's completely checked out.

What the fuck has happened to my Little Bit to cause this?

She's still staring blankly straight ahead and suddenly starts smiling, grinning, really.

I don't like this at all.

I tap on the window again a little harder; this time, she looks over at me with hazy, glassy eyes and fucking laughs.

"Open the door, Little Bit." I softly order her.

Upon hearing my voice, her smile and laughter fade. She's looking at me— through me— emotionless. She's completely disconnected. I want to gather her in my arms and bring her back to life. I want to be the person who does that for her.

"Please." I plead with her again to open the door. This time, she hits the unlock button, and I immediately react, opening the door and reaching over her to undo the seat belt and take the keys out of the ignition.

She's just sitting there, breathing heavily, seeing nothing. I scoop her little body out of the car, her arms hanging lifelessly at her sides, and carry her over to the picnic table.

118

I set her down on the top of it and stepped in between her legs to tilt her face up to look at me.

"Tell me what you need, darlin'," I smooth the hair away from her face and stroke her neck gently.

"What can I do for you?" I ask.

She takes a deep breath in and holds it; she holds it for so long that a flush rises to her neck and face. She finally lets it out and stares straight into my fucking soul.

And fuck if having her full attention doesn't do something to my insides. I've never felt so seen as when I'm with Charlotte.

"Zach." she breathes out like she's just realized I'm here with her.

"Yes, sweetheart, I'm here."

She reaches out and grabs the bottom hem of my muscle shirt, and pulls me towards her.

"Good." she wraps her arms around my waist and yanks me tightly against her in a firm embrace.

I am her lifeline at the moment; I know it's selfish to think about this in her time of despair but fuck, I like this. I like being needed by her. I like that she gets comfort from me.

I can't help myself as I wrap my arms around her neck until they fold over themselves, and I bury my face into the hair on the top of her head and give her feather-light kisses there.

We stay locked together for quite some time before I force myself to pull away just a little to check-in. She still hasn't said anything.

I thread my fingers through her silky blonde strands and gently tug her hair backward, letting her know I want to see her face.

She looks up at me, eyes searching my face.

Fuck, she looks so lost and hurt.

A tightness wraps around my chest, seeing her like this. Her smile is one of the best I've ever seen; her laugh is so sweet yet boisterous. And making her blush is quickly becoming my favorite thing to do.

It is so damn sexy to watch the flush start at her chest and creep its way up her milky neck and find home in those biteable cheeks.

I'm trying to be a good guy. I know she has a boyfriend; I've seen them together at school. They seem to be really into each other, and I respect that.

The thing is... I feel a connection with her that I can't explain.

Since the moment I first saw her falling apart in the woods, I wanted nothing more than to be the one to put her back together and make her happy.

A fool's errand? Perhaps.

It's hard for me to turn off my flirty charm, and I can't lie and say it hasn't helped me get into the beds of attached women before. In the year it's been since shit went down with Dani and my family, I went a little crazy.

I thought if I drowned myself in random pussy, I could forget about the hurt in my heart. Two families were destroyed that day, along with any potential future I had seen for us.

But this was different.

For the first time in a long time, I don't want to lose myself in Charlotte... I want to find myself.

Chapter 25

Thump, thump.

Thump, thump.

Thump, thump.

Breathe in. And out.

What are three things I see?

I turn my head to the right and see Zach's arm. He's sweaty, and he has goosebumps from the breeze up here. I look a little further, and I see my car. To the left of my car, I see a green power box sticking out of the ground. I turn my head back to his chest, pressing my forehead against it.

I close my eyes. What are three things I hear?

I hear the steady beating of Zach's heart. It's rhythmic and centering. I hear the whistling of the wind through the leaves, which are just starting to turn crunchy. I hear the faint whooshing of cars going by on the main road down below.

Eyes still closed. What are the three body movements I can feel?

I feel the rise and fall of my chest as my breathing starts to even out. I roll my shoulders forward and backward. Finally, I unclench my fists from Zach's shirt, slip my right hand underneath, and press my palm flat against his stomach. I ignore the sharp inhale of breath that comes from him, and

I slowly slide my hand upward, feeling the slick ridges as I go. I stop when I get to his hard, smooth chest and rest my hand against the muscle that now pounds rapidly like a hummingbird's wings.

He shudders at the touch, but I stay as I am. Eyes closed, forehead pressed against the middle of his chest, and my hand resting over his heart.

Breathe in. And out.

Again.

In and out.

Again.

"How do you feel, darlin'? Do you wanna talk about it?" Zach asks just above a whisper as he pulls back to bend down to eye level. He moves to sit beside me on the picnic table, our knees touching.

Do I want to talk about it? I'm not even really sure I understand it myself. But maybe it would be helpful just to tell someone what I'm feeling and see if an outside perspective might be able to shed some light on what I can do about it.

So, I tell him everything. From meeting Jason and falling hard and fast. How I was feeling jealous of Jade. Feeling guilty over Dean. How I was coping with losing my virginity. Jason's parents hating me. Savvy partying without me. Weird things I've noticed with my mom lately, and my mixed feelings on seeing my dad tonight. My ongoing nightmares. My conflicted feelings regarding himself and finally about the week-long rendezvous my boyfriend is having with his ex, and I haven't heard a fucking word from him.

We both remain silent for several minutes, sitting side by side. Zach lets out a puff of air and runs his hand through his hair. He turns to face me and grabs my hand, our eyes meet, and he starts to open his mouth, but no words come out.

I quirk a brow at him in silent question.

"That's... a lot to take in, baby girl." I nod my head in agreement and look down at my feet which are propped on the bench seat of the table. I move my foot over a rogue leaf; it's soft and partially brown. It's dying.

Me too, leaf. Me too...

He reaches over and hooks the bottom of my chin with his pointer finger, wanting me to look up at him again, "Can I just be honest with you?"

I nod and lean down to grab the dying leaf. Turning it over and over in my palms.

"Jade's fuckin' gorgeous," I choke on my next breath and look at him in disbelief; before I can say anything, he continues, "She's got a bangin' body, beautiful eyes, thick silky hair any man would wanna wrap his fists around. Lips that you can't help but imagine wrapped around your cock,"

I can't stop the tears from escaping, my voice is harsh and barely noticeable "Stop." I rasp, and he holds his hand up to stop me from interrupting. "She's tall with legs for days and an ass you could bounce a quarter off of."

I try to hold it in, but a loud sob escapes me. I press my hand to my chest to try to tamp down some of the pain as I watch my dying leaf float off into the breeze.

Zach stands and kneels on the bench in between my feet, gently grabs both sides of my face, and comes so close that I can feel his warmth across my lips. He uses both thumbs to catch some of the loose tears and move them away.

I squeeze my eyes so tight that it hurts and shake my head back and forth violently. I can't listen to this anymore. How has Jade bewitched both guys? Why am I constantly being made to feel inferior? It's bad enough that she's been with Jason in the past and possibly currently. *Fuck stop thinking about that.*

"Look at me, Little Bit." I don't, I can't.

His hands glide down to my neck, bracing each side as he places each thumb on my jawline and presses upwards. It's a gentle press but enough to tilt my face up a little.

"Open your eyes," he quietly demands while softly stroking my jaw.

I shake my head and feel more tears burning a hot path down my cheeks.

"Now, sweetheart."

My lids flutter open, my vision blurry from the collection of salty droplets.

"Now you listen to me and listen good. Even with all those things I just listed, Jade has nothin'," he grips me tighter, and his eyes darken to a mossy green as his stare intensifies. "Fucking *nothin'* on you, baby." I gasp but he continues like he didn't hear. "When you enter a room, everyone else disappears. Not only are you fuckin' heart-stoppingly beautiful on the outside, but you are so much more than that," he leans forward to touch his forehead to mine and closes his eyes.

He lowers his voice to a whisper, "God must've been showin' off when he created you, darlin'. You are genuine and kind. You feel with your whole heart—" his hand lands over the thumping organ, "and put everyone else first in your life no matter the cost to yourself. You are fierce and strong like whiskey in a teacup. There are millions of Jades in the world, but there is only *one* of you."

I make an effort to steady my breathing and swallow down the lump in my throat. "Jade may be pretty is as pretty does, bless her heart. But you, Little Bit, *you* set a man's fuckin' soul on fire."

I gasp at his declaration, and before I can even process what's happening, his lips are on mine.

Hard. Rough. I'm frozen for several seconds before I meet him back with equal fervor. His tongue swipes across my lower lip, demanding entry. I grant it.

His hands coast down my sides, landing on my hips as he pulls them forward until I have no choice but to wrap my arms around his neck and my legs around his waist or risk falling. He stands up and places both hands firmly on my ass to keep me upright.

We are a mix of lips, tongues, teeth and tears. A slight keening noise escapes my throat, and Zach lets out a gravelly moan. His grip on me tightens, and I press myself closer to him in response. I feel his hardness pressing against my core.

Fuck. *Fuck.*

What am I doing?

The fog lifts immediately, and I jerk my head back, "Put me down. Put me down, now!" my voice comes out high-pitched and panicky. He gently brings me down to the ground. "Shit, darlin' I'm sor..." I push his chest backward, cutting off his words and shaking my head.

"No." I turn away and run as fast as my legs will take me to my car. Zach is shouting behind me, but I don't stop or turn back towards him. I start the car and tear the fuck out of here.

What have I done?

Chapter 26

Fuck! What is wrong with me? How could I kiss Zach like that?

The road is barely visible through my tears. I'm going to crash the fucking car at this rate. The blurry but noticeable green and yellow Gas N' Go sign comes into view, and I whip into the parking lot, ignoring the honks from behind me. No doubt pissed at my lack of turn signal and brake usage. Whoops.

I park in front of the red brick building with the aluminum 'A' frame roof. Through the vestibule glass, I see the cashier Tiffany, a local community college student, open mouth smacking her Bubblicious and twirling a piece of her dirty blonde hair while boredly flipping through a magazine.

In through my nose for a four count. I hold my breath until my lungs are burning for air and clawing from inside their fleshy prison. *Out for an eight count through my mouth.*

She's blowing a big bubble.

In for four. Hold. Out for eight.

She's now picking the sticky substance off of the hot pink ball of her tongue ring.

In for four. Hold. Out for eight.

She has her tongue stuck out as far as it will go, her eyes going so crossed that it looks like they are trying to escape into her nose with her forefinger and thumb nails picking the gum off of the acrylic ball and a little bead of drool coming out of the left side of her mouth.

I giggle at the sight, and my shoulders release a little. Fucking Tiffany.

I head into the small convenience store and make a beeline for the back right corner. There, with its flashing lights and loud buzzing, stands my second favorite attraction in River View.

The Slurp-inator 3000. Funny enough, if the rumors are to be believed, that could also be a solid nickname for Tiffany.

I snort to myself as I grab the 44oz McKinley Gulp and begin to fill it with the only Slurpee flavor worth drinking. Blue-Motherfucking-Raspberry. If I'm feeling particularly fancy, I would add a healthy dollop of cherry right on top.

But today, it's all blue raspberry deliciousness.

I use the trick my mom taught me: take the big red straw, squish it flat to insert another one on top, and slide it halfway down, giving me an extra-long Slurpee straw. That way, I can use the round open lid and add a bit of extra liquid gold without losing my suction device to the overage.

I take my overly full beverage and head to the counter, grabbing a box of Raisinets along the way.

Tiffany is still picking out the last of the blown-out pinkness- maybe that's what they could call her instead- my chuckle at my own lame joke gets her attention.

"Sup' Charlotte. Who was that sexy piece of man meat I saw you with at the Coffee Hut the other day?" My brows furrow, and my lips twist in confusion. Sexy piece of what? What the hell is she talking about?

"That dude looked like he knew his way around some lady bits and could find the gooey center, if you know what I mean," she says with a smirk.

"You must be talking about Dean; I heard he's recently single and looking for some strange before he heads to college in the spring. If you want, I can pass along your digits?" I said sweetly. She doesn't need to know there's no way in hell I would sic a hotdog goblin like herself on sweet Dean. He may need to move on, but he doesn't need to ride the town bicycle to do so.

I typically try not to slut shame. To each their own and all that. Tiffany is hell on heels and wants any man who will look in her direction, taken or not. She has slept with a few of the girls I know from school's boyfriends.

Her current statement lets me know nothing has changed. If she saw me with Dean, she would've seen us hugging and talking. She didn't know if we were together or not, but here she was with her penis-fly-trap open and ready for insertion.

Tiffany grins like the she-wolf she is and presses a button on her little register. It spits out some extra receipt paper, and she starts writing. I take the paper and give her a syrupy sweet smile back. I leave a five on the counter and walk out.

I get settled in the car, and as I head towards the exit of the gas station, I see a portly trucker filling his tires with air. I grin evilly to myself as an idea forms.

I roll my window down, and I slow to a stop beside him, bent over with plumbers crack hanging out. "Hey, hot stuff," I shout to get his attention. He looks at me over his shoulder and takes me in from head to chest while licking his dry, gross lips. "What can I do ya for girly? You need some help?" The way he says 'help' makes my skin crawl.

I bat my lashes and reach the receipt out to him, "You know the hot blonde inside? She asked me to give you this and said if you were looking for a new 'lot lizard,' you'd know who to call. Whatever that means." His eyes widen in surprise as he looks towards the building where we can still see Tiff there, twirling her hair. He runs his stubby hands across his pot belly and fingers the hole in his grease-stained shirt where his belly button is.

Ugh, I've had enough. "Enjoy!" I shout as I drive away.

Chapter 27

My mind is swirling like a devastating tornado of emotional damage and self-loathing. I need to see Jason. I yank the car into the very next turnoff and flip around.

I pull up to his long, rocky driveway; all vehicles are present, so they must be back. Why would he not let me know they were back? He hasn't answered any calls or texts. Fuck I even sent him an email.

I grab my emotional support slushy and take a deep breath before exiting the car and heading to the front door, hyper-aware of the rocks crunching below the worn-out treads of my shoes.

I close my eyes and knock. I can hear someone coming and a deep sigh before the door opens with a whoosh, and I see the incredibly disapproving glare of Jason's dad, Neal.

His lips purse, and he rakes his judgey gaze over my appearance and tsks in distaste. He raises a brow at me and slightly leans his head forward. A silent "What the fuck do you want?".

I try for a sweet smile, "Hi, Mr. Donovan. Is Jason home?" I watch a wave of evil overtake him. His eyes darken, his posture straightens, and his nostrils flare. I'm surprised horns and a fucking tail don't sprout from this man. A slow smirk makes its way onto Lucifer's face.

He steps back and opens his arms into his home. A passing stranger might think I was having a warm welcome into a loved one's space.

I notice two things immediately. Number one is the utter silence in this house. It's very eerie and makes a chill run up my spine. The only person I see is Mr. Donovan.

There was clearly a party of sorts that occurred last night; there were red plastic cups on various surfaces. A big black garbage bag resting against the wall of the kitchen. Furniture moved against walls and out of the way to create an open gathering area.

The second thing I notice makes all the air leave the room. I don't understand what I'm looking at. I step forward toward the kitchen, where a very large "*CONGRATULATIONS JASON AND JADE!*" banner is tacked to the wall. Surrounded by red and gold balloons. On the table below, the banners are sweatshirts and lanyards with ASU Sun Devils on them.

What the actual fuck is happening.

A throat clears from behind me. A satisfied grin on his stupid fucking face as he tilts his head down the hallway towards Jason's room.

"Have at it," he says and walks away from me towards his office door, turning back and giving me a wink before he closes himself in the room.

I take a sip of my overfull slushy with shaking hands as I take a hesitant step towards my boyfriend's room.

It's okay. He will explain. I don't have all the information. His dad hates me, so he's probably making things seem worse than they are. But why didn't I know that Jason was applying out of state? Did he accept the offer? No. Stop it, Charlotte. Give him the benefit of the doubt.

He wouldn't have done anything without talking to me about it. This is all a big misunderstanding.

Another step.

I need to tell him I love him. I've waited long enough. He needs to make choices for his future, *our* future, with all of the information.

Another step.

I straighten my shoulders and shake my hair to my back. I smile to myself. I love him. I'm certain he loves me too. I can see it in those beautiful stormy eyes that melt my heart *and my panties*. I am going to walk in there, throw myself at him and tell him how much I love him, and seal it with a vagina hug.

I stop in front of his door. I can hear his heavy metal playing softly. I laugh to myself; he hates sleeping in silence. Notes of bergamot orange and the warm musk of his favorite incense cone, "Fresh Rain" come wafting out from the door frame.

I take a deep inhale of the signature scent of the one my heart loves and reach down to turn the doorknob.

Another step.

Entering the room, the blackout curtains are drawn, so it takes my eyes a moment to adjust. I blink hard a couple of times to try to get used to the lighting.

I wish I didn't.

I fucking wish God would take my eyesight right this second. I'm tempted to take this goddamn red straw and gouge out my own eyeballs. Pain be damned.

Nothing could hurt me worse than the sight before me.

My soulmate is lying peacefully on his side. Long black hair caressing his face, ever so slightly moving up and down with his inhales and exhales. His bare muscular torso greets my sight with a slight sheen of sweat —my man is a blast furnace when he sleeps. His sheets are tangled around his ankles. I look down at his bare feet. I love him so much that I even find his hairy man feet adorable.

My gaze travels up from those adorable feet to the mouth-watering gray sweatpants that hug his ass in all the right ways.

From that delectable ass, I continue my perusal up his rigid side to his shoulder, where he has the cutest cluster of freckles. I like to lick and nibble at that cute cluster.

Moving further down to his yummy biceps. The forearms do it for me in a way I never thought possible. The sinewy muscle that moves with every action of his hands or arms, *mmm, instant wetness.*

Speaking of hands, his are large and rough; they always make me feel small and delicate in the best ways. He is a true artist at heart, so he always has some kind of writing or drawing on the back of his hands or fingers.

The black doodles aren't what catches my attention today, though.

No, today I'm drawn to the way his large rough hand is only partly visible because the other half of it is below the thin, see-through, black mesh material of Jade's fucking underwear. Resting ever so protectively against what Zach described as "an ass you could bounce a quarter off of".

Chapter 28

What the fuck am I seeing here?

I can't seem to steady my eyes on anything in particular. They are on their own mission taking in the whole room. Clothes everywhere, his, hers, who fucking knows.

A mostly empty Jack Daniels bottle, crumpled tissues —gross—, a half unpacked suitcase, and random snacks. A bra is sitting on the top of the circular basketball-themed trash can. MY fucking bra that he took with him on his trip so he could "have something to remind him of me when he misses the hell out of me."

Fucking. Bastard.

I narrow my eyes back on Jason, my hand squeezes my McKinley Gulp, and a loud 'POP' occurs when the lid flies off. The noise must startle him because his eyes fly open. He stares at Jade's still sleeping form, draped over half his body in a lover's embrace. He gingerly pulls his hand out of her underwear and off her ass and ever so gently pulls his other arm out from under her. He reaches down to pull the sheet up, tucking her in and trying so hard not to wake her.

Once he's free of her body parts, he lays on his back, eyes closed, and exhales a deep breath while running his hand through his hair and massaging his scalp. He shakes his head free from whatever thoughts are running through it.

Nope, dear boyfriend, this is not an Etch-A-Sketch. Can't shake this away.

He rolls his body to the side, throwing his legs over the edge of the bed, and brings himself to a sitting position. His shoulders slump, and his head hangs as he leans over. He shakes his head back and forth again. I hear his sigh as he stands up, a crack of his knee, a telling sign that he's laid for too long in the same position.

He's looking down at the floor and kicks a pile of clothes out of the way, a bra that absolutely does not belong to me and his favorite band tee.

He looks up, takes a single step forward, and falters, eyes widening in disbelief.

We lock eyes. Nobody blinks. Nobody moves. Nobody breathes.

His lips part. My eyes dart to the lump that's cozied up in his bed. He turns his head, and his gaze follows mine. He immediately whips his head back in my direction and starts to reach for me.

No.

I run— barely feeling the cold ooze of the liquid sloshing around the rim of my cup with my steps.

"Charlotte!" he screams after me.

I hear a deep, rumbling laugh as I pass his dad's office door.

Fuck all these people.

My feet slap against the gravel, which feels slick like ice with each stride. I need to get out of here; in my haste, my keys fall to the ground, giving Jason enough time to catch up to me.

He grabs my shoulder to turn me back to him, "Baby, please." I've never seen his eyes so wild, his face so panic-stricken.

I have no emotion to give him right now. "Please, what, Jason? Are you about to spin me some bullshit like there's any possible fucking reason for you to be half naked, tangled in bed with someone who is not your goddamn girlfriend? Do you think I'm that fucking dumb?" my calm, even tone is surprising to my own ears.

I walk forward and get as close to him as I can without actually touching him. I don't want his tainted skin to touch mine ever again. I glare up at his stormy, glassy eyes and lift my chin. "Go on, *baby*, tell me those sweet lies. Explain this away."

He swallows hard and closes his eyes. His hands are fisted tightly at his sides. As they open, a tear falls. *Boo-fucking-hoo.*

"Jade's grandma died a few days ago. She was upset and crying, and she asked me if I would comfort her by holding her," he pauses, his eyes searching mine. For what? I have no idea. I have nothing for him right now. His delay is pissing me off. I wave my hand impatiently in front of me, urging him to continue his bullshit story.

He reaches for my hand and I jerk it away, "Don't fucking touch me. Keep going."

His body begins to shake slightly, and he flaps his hands at his sides— something he does when he's stressed.

"She laid in bed with me, and I held her while she cried. We had both been drinking..." he rushes out like the words themselves are burning down his insides.

My whole body goes cold, "Tell me nothing happened, Jason." He says nothing. "Jason. Tell me. Nothing happened, right?"

I stoically wait for him to answer.

Silence greets me. He has tears streaming down his beautiful face.

"Tell me!" I scream.

"I can't," he says so quietly I think I might have imagined it.

I feel like I'm having an out-of-body experience. Floating above the scene, just an innocent bystander. I watch myself keep my unwavering stare on Jason as my hand raises the McKinley Gulp. I watch Jason's eyes widen in knowing the exact moment I thrust the cup forward in his face.

I come back into my body, chuck the cup to the ground at his feet, and bolt for my car.

As I slam the door shut, I hear him scream my name again. I lock the doors, and my hands start to shake. Hot tears are now streaming down my cheeks.

I have to get the fuck out of here.

I miss the ignition as his hands slam against my window, I see him out of my periphery, but I refuse to look in his direction. Violent sobs are racking my body now and I try the ignition again, I drop the damn keys again when he tries to jiggle the door handle.

I lean down to pick them up and finally manage to get them inserted. I put the car in gear and slam my foot against the pedal. I hear the anguishing scream he lets out as I drive off.

I try not to, but I look in my rear view mirror and catch a glimpse of him, what a sight he is. All muscular, sleep-mussed, and shirtless... covered head to toe in Blue-Motherfucking-Raspberry slushy.

If I weren't so devastated, I would laugh. But right now? Right now, I kind of want to die.

A song comes on the radio as I drive away, something about being caught on the counter and banging on the sofa. I slam my fist into the power button. Bad fucking timing.

Chapter 29

There are times when living in a small town has its perks. This is one of them.

Did I really just catch my boyfriend in bed with another girl and then lose my fucking shit? On top of being the mother of all hypocrites directly before that, I let another guy stick his fucking tongue in my mouth.

I close my eyes hard and smash my head back into the headrest.

I keep smashing my head back and forth into the headrest, chanting "Fuck" over and over.

A light knock pulls me away from my self-flagellation as I turn towards the passenger window and see my bestie, two mugs in her hands. She motions to the lock with her head. I unlock it, and she climbs in.

She situates the mugs on the dash and turns her whole body towards me.

Sometimes I feel like we share the same brain. Savvy has a way of knowing what I need without words.

She reaches over and unclips my seat belt, pulls my elbow gently towards her until I fling myself at her and start sobbing in her arms.

She doesn't say anything; she knows this is all I need right now. Just a safe place to fall apart.

After what feels like forever of being comforted in my best friend's arms, her gentle rubbing of my back with her cheek resting on my head in silence, she starts rocking us back and forth softly and begins humming.

I'm focused on how our breathing has synced up and the calming repetitive motions of her petting when I start paying more attention to her humming.

I can start to make out the melody. I know this song. Something about liking Piña Coladas and dancing in the rain.

My shoulders start to shake with laughter, and I bite down playfully on her forearm.

"Are you really humming that song, Savvy?" I burrow further into her chest, which starts vibrating as her humming turns to belting out of lyrics.

"...And in the personal columns, there was this letter I read..." she pauses for dramatic effect, and when I don't respond, she pinches my love handle.

I manage a very loud yet muffled "IF YOU LIKE PIÑA CO-LADAS AND GETTIN' CAUGHT IN THE RAIN."

We sing the rest of the song, embracing just like that. My face buried, her stroking my hair as if I were Dr. Evil's cat.

After our impromptu American Idol audition, we both sit back with our lukewarm mugs in hand and stare blankly out of the windshield.

"So," she states expectantly. I'm surprised she gave me this long.

"Well, if you're wondering if Zach tastes like a starry summer night spent fireside eating s'mores with a hint of Watermelon Sour Patch Kids, the answer is yes. If you're wondering if Tiffany at the Gas'N'Go is still a skankalicious hoe-bag, the answer is also yes," I pause and examine my nails, "and if you're wondering what Jade wears when she's done fucking your boyfriend, I can confirm it is topless with a pair of black, slutty see-through underwear on." I say in the most casual of tones as if I were informing her of today's meteorological happenings.

Savvy calmly leans forward and sits her mug on the floorboard in between her bare feet and turns to full body face me, "Okay... we're going to put a pin in the Zach thing for a moment..." I look towards her and see that she's slowly removing her earrings, which she places in my empty cup holder.

She holds her hand out to me in a 'give me' motion, "Hair tie." she demands.

I tilt my head in confusion but hand over the black hair tie from my wrist. She proceeds to put her beautiful chocolate curls up into a bun on top of her head.

"Sav wha.."

She cuts me off by slicing her hand through the air; I blink back my surprise. She looks down at her ring-laden hands and begins to take them off. She has this particularly large gaudy one inscribed with the word '**BITCH**' in big bold letters that cross over her middle finger and ring finger of her right hand.

"You know what, better keep that one," she slides it right back on, tightens her bun once again, pulls her seatbelt across her body, and picks up her mug back up. "Okay, I'm ready, let's go."

"Uh, Savs, where are we going?" I question, thoroughly confused at what's happening.

"Oh, my dear sweet Charlie. You are going to drive us over to Jason's, where I am going to beat the ever-living shit out of them. I am going to rock Jade so hard that her grandchildren will be asking why grandma has 'BITCH' stenciled into her forehead. Now, shake a leg. Let's get it poppin'," she pats my thigh and faces forward with an evil grin on her face.

I lean my head forward on the steering wheel, close my eyes, and slump my shoulders. Against every one of my demands that they not, the tears begin to fall.

Arms wrap around me, and we sit in silence for just a moment.

"Oh, Charls, do you want me to kill them? I know people. And come on, this is Alaska; there are so many places to hide their two-timing, piece of shit bodies," she asks so sweetly; I can't help but smile.

She pulls back and brushes my hair away from my face, "But seriously, are you okay? What can I do?" her voice quivers, and I instantly feel guilty for putting my drama on her. I know Thanksgiving is always a rough time for her. When she was really young, her dad was killed by a drunk driver on his way home from the grocery store with the holiday meal.

"Go somewhere with me?" I ask.

"Anywhere."

* * *

The wind howls to my right. I close my eyes and twist my left shoe into the loose sediment below it. Distantly I can hear the roar of an airboat as it coasts down the river in front of me.

At the mouth of the river, a family is unloading their two dogs. One large, furry, and dark brown. One small, white, and hardly any fur. The little one seems too small to be out in this brisk wind.

Also, I've seen a Bald Eagle take off with prey larger than this little scamp, so the Mrs. better keep a keen eye out for sky-bears.

We've made a little hovel on our side of the river. This is the side that's less for exploring because the terrain is so unforgiving and unpredictable.

My mom's poor car would've sunk for sure, so we've hoofed it to find the perfect place to set up.

We hiked, well 'hiked' is a generous term for stumbled and narrowly fell into the brush, rushing water, and a fire pit on our hunt for a perfect spot.

Camping chairs, tidied in their bags, strung across our backs. Our breaths come in pants as we struggle to walk through the deep, unsteady, crushed rock and silt.

We found a little cluster of trees, leaves long since died and drifted off to their next destination. It blocks a little of the sharp wind, just a little.

It's now that I find myself looking at the other side of the river —the visitor-friendly side. I can't help but feel like this is a representation of my life.

Always on the outside looking in. Present, but not belonging. Watching the things I want be just on the other side of attainable.

I turn my face towards the wind and revel in the large bursts that steal my breath like a thief in the night. If I hold my head in this position, I just might suffocate.

There's something almost peaceful about that thought.

The wind is so strong, cold, and intense that my eyes sting with the tears being forced to wet my battered globes.

I blow out a long breath, trying to expel the dangerous

thoughts swirling around inside my mind.

How is this my life right now? Was I some giant piece of shit in a past life? Do I deserve this extreme karmic punch in the gut?

"It'll be alright, you know," she states with a light kick of her foot against mine; it's not a question.

I turn to face her, blinking back those burning tears. The tears are trying their hardest to rip themselves from my body; not even my own fucking tears can stand to be with me.

"Will it, though, Savs? 'Cause right now, I feel like nothing will ever be alright again."

If only I knew then that things could and would get worse. So much worse.

Chapter 30

I lay in bed, staring blankly at the ceiling. No sounds to be heard except the groaning of this 1970s split-level we live in. Mom took off to pick up my dad, and I faked being asleep when she popped in to see if I wanted to go.

Don't get me wrong, I missed him, but I just cannot bring myself to "people" right now.

My head is a mess. I've been steadily ignoring the buzzes of my phone, signaling the seventh. No, make that *eighth* missed call from Jason.

Silence once again takes over the room, only for a moment.

One solid buzz lets me know there's now a message to accompany the many missed calls.

Jason: We need 2 talk.

I grip my phone tight, so tight I hear the plastic bending under the pressure. I have the biggest urge to hurl the fucking thing at the wall.

Talk? Fuck you. What else needs to be said? He clearly hasn't been open and honest with me regarding our future and his plans otherwise. That and just the little fact that he cheated on me and then tried to explain it away.

I get that I'm not innocent and that I did Jason dirty when I kissed Zach back. I'm not trying to excuse my behavior, and I had every intention of telling Jason what happened and begging for his forgiveness.

And I stopped. I fucking *stopped*.

I'm not blind or naive, I know Zach and I have a connection. I have consciously chosen to ignore it and place him squarely in the friend zone. I don't want to lead him on or give him hope of something more. Well, I didn't mean to, but it looks like I fucking failed spectacularly at that today.

Fuck my life.

But Jason didn't stop. He betrayed me in the worst way. Without a thought to how this would impact me and our lives. He's fucking selfish. I told him. I *told* him that Jade was being shady, that she still wanted him, and that it made me uncomfortable.

Maybe he knew all along. Maybe I'm just a big joke, and he's been fucking her the whole time. I can't trust anything now. How could I be so stupid? Did I miss the signs?

Not for the first time tonight, I think about the last year of my life.

This was supposed to be such an exciting time for me and my friends. Senior year of high school, our lives wide open ahead of us.

Colleges, careers, parties, and sex. Being adults, carving our own paths, making our own rules. Everything would be great. Everything would be better. Everything would be happy. *I* would be happy.

I never allowed myself to think of a scenario where things could completely fall apart. This was the happy chapter I was chasing, the one that kept me from being completely consumed by darkness. The light at the end of the tunnel.

Now what?

As I lay in the pitch-black of my bedroom, I squeeze my eyes closed tightly until white patches appear behind my lids. When I open them, I can make out those patches on the ceiling, and in the static, I can create my own images.

A picture starts to form of sitting back at the top of Sky Ridge. Except this time, there are no tears. No beautiful tan boys with hypnotic green eyes. No barriers. Nothing stopping me.

I stare straight out of the windshield, and my eyes follow a cluster of dried leaves blowing by in the near distance to a raven perched on the thin branch of a dying Birch.

I see the wood sway underneath the raven's weight. His feathers are so black they take on a blue hue, eyes so dark they peer into my chest and attempt to snatch my soul from my body.

"Caw, caw, caw," he sings to the wind.

It's like he's counting down for me.

"Caw." *One.* I tighten my left hand on the steering wheel while my right hands rest snugly against the gear shift, thumb poised on the button to the side.

"Caw." *Two.* My thumb depresses the button, and I shift down to 'Drive' with three audible clicks.

Once the third click sounds, my right hand joins its counterpart on the steering wheel.

My fingertips feel the rigid stitching of the leather pieces. I press them harder, knowing if I pulled them away to look, I would see the stitch pattern now etched into my skin.

"Caw." *Three.* My right foot lifts from the brake pedal and eases onto the gas pedal.

When I pictured this scene before, I slammed my foot on the gas and soared over the ledge like a total badass — Thelma and Louise style.

But not this time.

This time, everything slows down.

My eyes don't leave the raven. He doesn't blink, and neither do I.

Not until my car slams into the cement barrier; the barrier is meant to stop this exact thing from happening, but instead, that barrier disintegrates as if it's made of ash.

As the car careens over the ledge of the tall peak, my body floats above the chaos, and I watch the small sedan flip once… twice… three times … before landing amongst a cluster of Pine and teetering back and forth unsteadily.

The wind chose that moment to pick up, and a well-placed gust thrusts the car forward, where it does two more flips.

"Caw."

My eyes dart back to the mysterious feathered creature. He continues to stare at me with those midnight eyes. As he blinks, I feel more than I hear the enormous BOOM that fills the air, immediately capturing my attention once more.

Flames shoot out of the now broken windows of the mangled car, I can feel the heat dancing on the breeze bringing with it a rancid smell of metal and sulfur.

I can't look away from the devastation below.

My ears perk up to the sound of flapping as the raven takes flight. The scene below becomes darkened like a vignette is being placed around it.

There's a certain beauty in the chaos, and terrible things can be beautiful. Here in the darkness of my room, all things are possible.

It's with this fantasy etched in my mind that I drift off to sleep with a resigned, tired smile on my face.

Chapter 31

"Charlie Bear," a soft voice coos. I feel the bed dip as a warm body lays down next to me. Before I even open my eyes, I can tell it's morning with the amount of light streaming in from behind my lids.

"Ch–Ch–Charlie Bear," he coos again, adding a light finger stroke from the crease of my forehead to the tip of my nose.

"Wakey, wakey, my sweet Charlie Bear." A giant smile spreads on my face, and I let my eyes flutter open to see the best man I've ever known. The only one to never hurt me. The one I place my full trust and faith in. My dad.

We turn to face each other, one arm tucked under the now shared pillow; the other arm curled in front of our respective chests.

"Hi, Daddy," I rasp, voice dry from the night. "I missed you so much. I'm glad you're here."

A sweet smile spreads on his face as he claps his palm over my mouth, "And I missed you, my sweet girl, but before we continue any additional conversation, I'm going to need you to get your butt up and brush your teeth." he lets out a huge sigh and places a dramatic hand across his forehead. "Thank God I was lying down when your rank morning breath graced my nose. Otherwise, I fear I might've passed out." he teases.

"Hardy-har-har, you are hilarious, Mr. Johnson." I roll my eyes, but I do get a whiff of my breath, and he's totally right, so I jump out of bed and rush to the bathroom.

When I emerge clean and ready for the day, I see my dad sitting on the loveseat with the Macy's parade playing on the TV. I plop myself beside him, he lifts his arm to reveal the perfect Charlie shaped opening. I snuggle against his side and just breathe him in.

I haven't seen him since last Christmas. We talk often, but being in his orbit is a very different experience. I hate that our family is scattered to almost the far corners of the US. It's been a long time since my parents split, but they've never made us feel like less than a family. If it weren't for their careers, I think they would both be on board to live in the same area just so we could spend more time together as a unit.

When I see how they interact, I can't imagine what could've made them want to call it quits. They have great chemistry. They joke and laugh all the time. I'm not crazy, I know there had to be something to tear them apart but when I've asked, they both pretty generically say the same thing, "We just grew apart".

I do know that at the time, Mom was working towards a promotion, and she was under a lot of pressure. While she struggled to climb the corporate ladder, my dad seemed to fly past every milestone in his company.

He was given accolade after accolade, promotion after promotion. He was sent as the company ambassador to close some very lucrative deals. They even gave him his own personal assistant.

I wonder if that created resentment between them. I feel like you would want your partner to succeed no matter what, but I guess I could see how it might be hurtful to see someone appear to have it so easy while you're working your ass off for very little payoff.

Even though it's been almost eight years since they divorced, I can't remember a time leading up to D-day that explains it.

They bickered, sure, but never yelled. No aggression, no violence, no snarky comments, or obscene facial expressions.

We were a happy family, and then one day, they walked into my room side by side and crushed my world.

Even their divorce was quick, easy, and friendly. They didn't fight over any material objects. They immediately agreed on a custodial plan for me, with my input, of course.

It just doesn't make sense.

Are all relationships just doomed to fail? Is that the lesson in all of this?

My dad bumps my ribs gently with his hand, "Thinking awful hard for a bright holiday morning, baby girl." I lean my head on his chest and let out a soft sigh. "Sorry, Dad, it's been a rough week."

"You know what might make it feel better?" he asks with a quirk of his eyebrow. Before I can respond, he pats my arm and jumps off the couch. Like literally jumps and clicks his heels together like a leprechaun. I shake my head and let out a full belly laugh.

"Madam," he returns to the couch with one arm bent across his stomach with a dish towel placed on it, like a proper waiter, his other hand fluttering a tray in front of my face.

"Oh, Mom is so going to murder you!" I whisper shout as I grab one of the bacon-crumbled adorned deviled eggs. My mom's favorite thing to make —and eat— for special occasions. She is very protective over them, though. She always gets an accurate count of guests and allows exactly three deviled eggs per guest. No more, no less.

The tell-tale creak of the floorboard from the hallway captures my attention, and Dad's eyes widen to a comical size. I shove the entire egg in my mouth as she says, "What are you two up to, hm?" Dad has scurried away like the traitor he is, no doubt to hide his involvement in what is sure to be known as "Egg-gate 2005" for years to come.

"Mufphin ohm!" I fail amazingly at saying 'Nothing, Mom' with a full mouth of stolen eggy goodness. I hear the traitor who gave me half of my DNA snicker from behind me.

"Mmhm, guys, can we save the weirdness for at least when it's acceptable to pop a bottle of wine?" she asks, pretending to be exasperated with us, but I see the small smile on her lips.

Dad winks at me and puts his arm around Mom's shoulders, "You got it, Ellie. Nothing but best behavior from here on out." he holds up three fingers in 'Scouts Honor'. *Lies!* He was never a scout. I giggle to myself but try to keep my face serious and nod my head emphatically in agreement.

* * *

As we sit around the cramped table, stuffed full of all the holiday staples, I look at each of my loved ones' faces. Everyone is smiling, laughing, telling stories. I'm trying my hardest to remain present. To not think about the absolute dumpster fire my life has become. I left my cell at home because I just needed one day. One fucking day where I feel like I could maybe make it through all this. Where I don't feel like I'm drowning, drifting away at sea with no chance of rescue.

I feel my mood plummet. Sometimes the change is noticeable to me, sometimes it's not. Today I can feel the cold wave of indifference settling over me like a second skin.

I catch Savvy's stare from across the table, she's leaning forward with her chin resting in her palm and she taps her forefinger twice against her cheek. Our secret signal for "all good?". I shake my head slightly.

No Savvy, it's not all good, and I don't know if it ever will be.

I have to try, for my parent's sake, to hold on to any shred of happiness that I can. They don't deserve a broken mess of a child.

Don't worry, Mom and Dad. In this, I have a lot of practice. I've been fooling people for years.

So, I straighten my shoulders, fling my hair over my shoulder, paste on the best smile I can muster, and join in on the conversation. Trying to ignore the concern written all over my bestie's face.

Chapter 32

I think we overdid it this year. I look across my living room, completely covered with random bags and products from our very successful day of combat shopping, aka Black Friday shopping. I feel like I've come back from going two rounds with Mike Tyson.

We were packed like sardines in the stores; elbows were thrown, and people were shoving and kicking. People breathing their hot, nasty breath down my neck. Many were ready to fully throw hands over the last 24ct plastic Tupperware set.

It was amazing and invigorating. I got in an old lady's face.

Before you judge me, just know that I was first in line for the newest model of a highly sought-after brand of computer. I did what you were supposed to do on Black Friday, I prepped. I went through the ads; I decided what was most important to me and I had a plan. By the time we got to the store to stand in line for opening, we were handed a brochure with a map of the locations of certain items. I cross-referenced that map with my list of wants and made my battle plan.

Well, little Gertrude decided to say fuck Black Friday etiquette and wander up to where I was placing *my* computer into *my* cart and tried to take it out of my hands. I was initially polite, respecting elders and all that. Delores growled at me, fucking growled like a withering coyote, and tried to take it again, with more oomph this time.

Hell to the no.

"Ma'am, this is my computer. I waited for it, and I will be taking it." I warned.

She refused to let go, "Well, there are no more, and I promised my grandson I would get him one." Not my fucking problem, Edith! I pulled the box more to my chest and leaned over the top.

"Well, I guess you've got an apology to work on; now, if you'll excuse me and let go, I need to head out."

Beatrice clearly wasn't ready to throw in the towel as she pulled the box more towards her chest and yelled, "You'll have to pry it from my cold, dead hands!"

Now, I was raised right. I do try to show people respect, even before they've earned it. I have manners, and I use them. Please, thank you, all that jazz. But you know what? Evelyn can get fucked. Enough is enough.

I leaned as close to her face as I could get, inhaling the sickening scent of mothballs and rose water with such an intense level of malice that I surprised myself as I bit out, "Lady, your hands are already cold, and if you really want me to make them dead too, we can arrange that. Let the fucking box go and step away."

She instantly dropped her hands and gaped at me; I offered her a bright smile and a wiggle of my fingertips as I turned the cart around and shouted over my shoulder, "Have a lovely day, Agatha!" I could see her clutching whatever cheap version of pearls she had hanging around her wrinkly neck.

I look across the bounty strewn all about the room and snicker at the memory. I felt bad at first, but you know what, fuck that. If, at her age, she still has no manners or common courtesy, then the bitch needs to find out she won't be extended any either.

* * *

The holiday break went by too fast for my liking. I miss my dad already. When we dropped him off at the airport yesterday, it took everything in me to let him go. I know he'll be back at Christmas for another visit, but it just feels too far away.

It took great effort to get myself out of bed this morning. I couldn't even muster enough care to put on my armor.

No, instead, I rocked up to school in what Savvy calls my "Bobos": An old pair of tattered light wash, high-waisted jeans and a threadbare, holey Care Bear shirt with fuzzy socks in a pair of faded black and white Adidas slides. I have zero makeup on save for a touch of ChapStick because one should never neglect one's mouth.

No matter how I feel, I never want to subject myself to the scaly creature my lips turn into without it being exposed to the Tundra-esque conditions of the Great North.

"Well, you look like shit." a light, airy voice sounds from behind me. Savs. I shrug my shoulders and give her a grunt in return. I love her to death, but sometimes she just has the worst timing. Can't she tell I just fucking can't right now? I feel like I'm sinking into a dark hole with no hope of the stars lighting my way back.

"Charlie, turn around," she demands.

I shake my head back and forth. Come on, Savs, just let me be.

"Charlie, I am your daddy. Be a good girl and do as I say." she retorts in her best —which is terrible— Darth Vader voice.

A ghost of a smile makes its way onto my face against my wishes, I shake my head again and cluck my tongue, "That's not how that saying goes, Savs."

"Um yeah, I'm pretty sure it is... Or was that the start of a porno? Same diff." I hear her sigh and feel her shoulder pressing up against mine, "Fine, then I'll stay here too." Of course she will, because no matter what, she's always been my person. The one I can count on for everything. Even though she may not fully understand my periods of darkness, she wades through it with me, ready to punch whatever monsters lurk in the blackness right in the junk.

I peek slightly to the left to see her mirroring my position. Arms draped lifelessly at her sides, forehead pressed firmly against the cool metal of someone's locker, eyes closed with a spot of condensation that comes and goes with her breath against the dark maroon.

Her posture is shit. I'm pretty sure she's mimicking me in that regard as well. But she's so dramatized about it that she appears something akin to Quasimodo. If I cared more, I would fix my stance and tell her to suck it.

"What time is it, Charlie?"

A grunt is my only audible response. She's trying to coax me out of my doom and gloom with a familiar calling.

She elbows me impatiently in the ribs, "I said, what time is it?"

"Fuck you, Savs," I respond with a chuckle and an elbow back to her ribs. A little call and response is not going to magically fix my mood.

"Bitch, tell me what time it is!" she shouts. She's not going to let this go.

"Ouch*!*" I hiss loudly when I feel a hard slap to my barely protected ass.

"It's time to put my big girl panties on and take care of business…" I mumble so she'll shut the fuck up and quit drawing attention to us.

But, that's not good enough for Savannah Mitchell, oh no.

"I couldn't quite hear you, Charlie; what was that?" she cups her ear in my direction with her other arm extended in a flourish towards the slowly expanding audience we've amassed. She's most comfortable in the limelight, putting her years of cheer to good use, voice booming and words in a staccato rhythm.

You know what? Fuck it. I spin around and fling my head forward, gathering my hair together in my hands and putting it in a tight bun with a sassy 'oomph'.

Fake it til' you make it, Charlie. You know better than anyone else how to be fake and make people believe what you want them to.

I cup my mouth with both hands and bellow out, "I said it's time to put on my sexy, lacy big girl panties and take care of some mother fucking business!"

I'm met with hoots, hollers, and catcalls from all directions from boys and girls alike, and even a few… marriage proposals?

I howl with laughter next to my bestie, who is now putting on her best "I'm better than you, and you know it," gaze across the crowd. She points her finger at some underclassman, I think his name is Todd? Trent? Travis maybe?

"You there, come forth." He stands stock still, starstruck by the beautiful woman who is placing her attention directly on him. He looks like he might throw up or run away and hide under the bleachers until the end of school bell. Poor guy. He seems to shake off a bit of his apprehension and slowly steps forward.

"We've chosen you..." she waits for him to fill in the blank with his name with an impatient wave of her hand.

"Uh, T-Tim..." he sputters, heat blooming in his soft, full cheeks.

"Ah, yes. Dear sweet Timmy, gather our things if you would be so kind as to follow your Matriarchs thusly."

I can't help my laughter from bubbling out at her ridiculousness. As crazy as her request is, Timmy is nothing but eager to follow her edict. His chest puffs out with pride as he lifts her cheer bag on one shoulder and my crossbody on the other.

Suddenly, my breath leaves my body as I watch the ground become smaller and feel warm, rough hands banding around each thigh, with another set around my waist to steady me. I reach both hands out to each of my sides, and they both land on two very different sets of hair.

I look down at the two football players who have hoisted each of my ass cheeks onto one of their shoulders. The player to my right, with the long dreads braided down his broad back. The number "23" on his back and "Whitaker" splayed across his shoulders.

I grip his braid and give it a playful tug. He smiles up at me, and I grin back, "Onward, Maxi!"

"Fuck yeah, baby, whatev..." he starts to respond but is cut off by a growl to my left, "Watch your mouth, Whitaker. She deserves more than that. We will follow you anywhere, my Queen."

Though I recognize the low, gravelly voice, my brain cannot comprehend who it came from. I grip his sandy hair with shaky fingers and gently tug backward. As I suspected, I am met with those striking green orbs.

All I can manage is a nod, an unspoken acceptance of his words. He squeezes my thigh, and we move forward as a unit.

Chapter 33

Winter 2005

These last couple of weeks have been hell. I barely sleep; Mom is constantly hovering over me and threatening to force-feed me if necessary. I've dropped at least eight pounds since Thanksgiving.

When I do manage to get more than a couple of broken hours of sleep, it's plagued with nightmares of varying depictions rolling on a highlight reel. Most often some form of Jason and Jade fucking like wild animals. In positions that I can only imagine came straight from CornHub's top requested AVN award-winning videos.

Sometimes, for an extra special session of torture, Zach joins them, and the three of them whisper conspiratorially about how fucking dumb I am for not seeing it sooner or a myriad of insults to my sexual prowess versus the apparent erotic queen herself with the vagina made of beer, football stats, and gold.

As if that's not enough to make me want to gouge out my own eyeballs and bathe my brain in bleach, occasionally, I have the raven dream.

That one is always the same, though. The crash, the feel of the flames, the acrid smell of rotten eggs, and just a dash of sweet maple syrup permeating the air, the judgment of the raven's eyes. Always the same.

That one haunts me the most. I wondered what the symbolism might be beyond the obvious death implications. I pulled up the AskReeves website on my new computer —*thanks, Florence!*— and asked the powers that be what the presence of a raven could mean in a dream.

I shouldn't have looked it up, though I'm not shocked to find that the first four reasons you may see a raven in your dreams are a sign of betrayal, misfortune, death, and sorrow. Cool.

* * *

I stand at my locker gathering my Trapper Keeper, favorite gel pens, and textbook, eager to get this last class over with. I am beyond ready for the two-week Christmas break. My fingers grip the top of the metal door, and I gaze down at the few photos stuck to its matte surface.

A smiling picture of Savvy and me from the first day of our Freshman year. We wore matching hairstyles, a horrific mix of side ponytails and barrel bangs —gross. It was a true assault to the sight of those who came into contact with us, but we couldn't have cared less. We were on top of the world. Ready for the next chapter, ready to "grow up" and take on the world.

We were fucking idiots.

Below that gem is a picture of my parents and me taken last summer at the Fourth of July fireworks display at Bear Park in downtown River View. If I close my eyes, I can still hear the murmur of a crowd, the tings of footfalls along the gravel reminiscent of broken glass, a heavy aroma of sweetness on the breeze from the funnel cake booth, and the magnificent, booming display of firework smoke. The fireworks would've been hella more impressive if the sky was actually dark enough to see them.

But alas, Alaska is the land of the Midnight Sun, and we know three things for sure: you will probably have to wear a snowsuit over your Halloween costume; we don't have "Summer," we have "Construction."; you will not see a magically colorful fireworks display for the fourth of July, you have to wait for New Years for that spectacle.

Fireworks have always captivated me. The complexity of viscerally shedding its skin with an incandescent chemical bath.

A precise mixture of propellant and charge followed by an ignition is used to create enough force to allow the gasses to escape in one direction and push the fireworks in the other. Then boom, *magic*.

If fireworks can teach us anything, it's that sometimes you have to burn and suffer before the rebirth to a state of peaceful beauty. Like a Phoenix rising up to be brighter, stronger, and with a purity it didn't possess in the lives that came before.

Being reborn from the ashes means you know what it's like to die inside. Maybe that's why I feel drawn to the fiery presentation. I, too, know what it feels like to die inside while putting on a brilliant show to those who are none the wiser of the combustion occurring within.

I let out a slow breath and close my locker door, twisting the combo lock twice to re-engage the mechanism. Not that it matters. I don't have anything of value in my locker, especially not the tattered metal band hoodie tucked haphazardly in the back. I can't bring myself to touch it for fear of what feelings the scent of the boy I love, who cut me so deep with betrayal, will bring forth.

"Hey Charlie, do you have the worksheet due today for Mr. Steiner's class?" a semi-familiar baritone timbre comes from my left.

Ezekiel Fox, "Zeke", one of River View High's most sought-after running backs and self-proclaimed Lothario. My eyes roll so hard I'm almost concerned they will never find their way back to the center.

"Zeke, when was the last time you turned in *anything* in Steiner's class? That man worships at your ginormous stinky ass feet. Everyone knows players skate, and you don't need to do shit to pass." I grip my textbook a little tighter and press forward through the throng of people filling the hallways.

Not to be deterred by my prickly dismissal, Zeke falls in step with me again. He lifts a loose tendril from my now messy bun and twirls it around his meaty finger. A chill of disgust works its way up my spine.

"So I heard the Freakazoid went back to banging Gothic Barbie, and you're fair game again."

I come to a screeching halt and slowly turn to face him fully. His cocky smile and swagger pisses me off further. I cock my head slightly to the side, narrowing my eyes and keep my tone low, dangerous, "What the fuck did you just say to me?"

He is completely unphased by the murderous intent floating between us like a thick fog.

With complete disregard for his own safety, this dickhole opens his mouth again, "Well shit Charlie, everyone knows you finally gave up that cherry pussy, and he threw it back out for the rest of us to have a taste."

I watched a movie once where the main character described falling into a red mist before doing something extremely violent. I've never understood that feeling more in my life than I do at this moment.

I don't even think, I lunge forward, fist raised and bring it down hard on his nose. I try not to cringe at the sickening crunch and immediate onslaught of blood cascading down his surprised face. I watch in shock at my own actions as the surprise on his face slowly morphs into a mask of pure fury.

Before he's able to move a muscle, a voice booms above the cacophony of sound in the busy hallway.

"Mr. Fox, how about you visit the nurse and have her take a look at your face? Next time be more careful to pay attention to where you're walking," Mr. Clarke states with an eyebrow raised, challenging Zeke to say something else caused his injury. "Ms. Johnson, my office. NOW!".

Fuck.

I quickly follow our Principal into his office. He motions for me to take one of the black leather chairs while he sits opposite behind his mahogany desk.

"Miss Johnson, care to explain to me what the hell I just witnessed out there?" he asks in exasperation, removing his thick, black plastic eyeglasses and pinching the bridge of his nose while squeezing his eyes shut.

I avert my gaze to the placard on his desk *Philip Clarke, Principal.* It's a black lacquer set atop a nice brick of cherry-colored wood. It looks sturdy, heavy, like I could go back and smash it into Zeke's stupid fucking face again. He won't be so hot after that, would he? Asshole.

Mr. Clarke clears his throat, clearly waiting for my response.

I don't really know what to say. "Charlotte, I have known you for most of your school career, and I have never seen such behavior from you. I know that Ezekiel is what you kids call a "fuck boy," and to be honest, it made me a little proud to see you stand up to him. However, you cannot go around letting your fists do the talking."

I nod dejectedly along. He's right. I know I shouldn't have hit Zeke. I'm used to his boorish demeanor and insensitive conversational skills. I'm usually quick to give it back as good as I get it. But when he said that shit about Jason, the red mist descended.

How did he even know that we've had sex? Surely Jason didn't tell people. Or did he? Fuck, I don't even know him like I thought I did.

"I'm sorry, Mr. Clarke. I truly am. I don't know what came over me. Normally, I can ignore his witless behavior, but today, he just set me off."

He sighs and grabs his glasses, putting them back on the perch of his nose, and looks down at me with something akin to sympathy, maybe pity, "I should call your mother and suspend you. An act of violence like this, we could take away your ability to attend the prom and possibly the ability to walk across the stage for your diploma in the spring..."

My heart starts beating at an unnaturally high rate; it feels like I've stuck my head out of the window while driving 100 MPH, and all the air has left my lungs. Before I can sputter out any pleas and begging, he starts speaking again.

"But I will not do any of that. You are a good student Charlotte. You have never been trouble, and I trust this is an isolated incident, never to be repeated, correct?" he pins me with that intense, authoritative stare.

I nod enthusiastically, "Y-yes, sir, I promise. Never again. Thank you so much, sir. I appreciate it more than you know."

He leans back in his chair, a ghost of a smile on his lips, "How is the hand?" he tips his chin in the direction of the swollen, throbbing right hook in question.

I flex it and wince a bit at the ache. "It's a bit sore, but I'll be okay."

He shrugs and begins to stand " Yes, I suspect you will be Miss Johnson. Why don't you gather your belongings and head out? Get an early start on the break."

"Oh, I still have Chem.." He cuts me off before I finish, "I am aware of your class schedule, but seeing as it is the last day and I happen to know it is movie day so you will not be missing anything of significance. I will let Mrs. Kelley know that your absence is excused. Now get out of here before I change my mind."

 He doesn't have to tell me twice; I am so ready to get the fuck out of here. I nod rapidly and gather my things and begin to leave his office, as I twist the knob to let myself out he says, "And Charlotte? Get some ice on that hand." I look back at him and nod once as I close the door, "Yes, sir."

Chapter 34

I can't believe the break is halfway over already. I've spent most of it in my room. When I came home from school early, I wasn't really prepared to explain to Mom how and why my knuckles were busted and swollen.

As a rule, I don't lie to her. We keep communication open and honest. Which makes me feel a small pang of remorse when I think about the ridiculous fucking lie I told her when I got home.

For some reason beyond my comprehension, she just couldn't wrap her head around the possibility that my backpack strap got stuck in between the metal bracket attaching it to the door, and when I pulled on the strap —very hard, mind you— it suddenly gave way, and my hand ended up scraping against the metal lip of the door.

Complete freak accident. As for why I was early, that was simply the truth. The Principal witnessed the damage occur and agreed to let me head out early since nothing was pressing in the final class of the day.

It turns out that when you spend your life being open and honest with someone, they are keenly aware of when you are full of shit.

She didn't really press me for anything else; she just highly suggested I spend my upcoming days working on college essays, getting a head start on readings and assignments due, and really think about the "direction my life is going."

To my surprise, not only did I follow her "suggestion," but I got a ton accomplished. I haven't experienced much adversity in my life, so my essay was extremely lacking. I wrote and rewrote it so many times. It was all shit.

Finally, at like 3 am, while I was staring at the ceiling, throwing a crumpled piece of paper up and down and contemplating just saying fuck college altogether, I can just ride the rails and live in shanties around the world. I had a bit of an epiphany.

There is one thing that I've had to constantly overcome for as long as I can remember. Myself.

I'm self-aware enough to know a few intrinsic truths.

I know it's not 'normal' how my moods can shift drastically in a short time period. Sometimes, I'm aware of the shift; sometimes, it's a complete shock.

I know I think about my end probably more than is healthy, if there even is a healthy amount of thinking about killing yourself.

I know I've gotten so good at hiding myself behind the 'chill girl' persona that no one really knows the real me. There is a different, watered-down version of Charlotte that's been carefully cultivated and built for each individual in my life.

So that's what I wrote about. My experience dealing with fighting my own mind, trying to overcome my own instinct to self-sabotage.

Of course, I fluffed it up in a nice shiny package. I don't think I can truly list out the darkness that exists in my psyche without someone coming in a white unmarked van to strap me up and throw me into a padded room.

Feeling better that I finished that little masterpiece last night, I let myself sleep in a bit this morning. I find it a bit odd that I didn't get Mom's special wake-up, which has become customary over the last week.

Instead of decorating the house in one sitting, Eleanor Johnson thought she'd add to her subtle punishment by waking me up at seven fucking fifteen in the morning to do some decorating here and there.

My dad was unable to secure a flight to be here by Christmas day, so we decided as a family to celebrate New Year's and Christmas together.

So T-minus three days until the Johnson Family Christmas!

My bladder is giving me a big middle finger for not getting up to empty it in way too long after chugging a two-liter of soda to get a little more caffeine in to finish my essay last night.

I groan as I roll off my bed, curling my toes into the plush carpet below as I stretch my arms high over my head. I grab the plush plaid PJ pants off of my computer chair and hop from one foot to the other, narrowly avoiding falling on my face to put them on.

My tongue is glued to the roof of my mouth, the atmosphere is as if a desert and a cat box had a baby, and that baby took a shit in my mouth, and that shit sat for forty days and forty nights in the blistering heat. *Gag.*

Must brush teeth now.

I slip my slides on and make my way to the bathroom door. I can see the small vanity light is on and a big shadow against the bottom of the door.

As I lift my hand to knock, I hear a faint sniffle. I let my hand fall to the wood and rap a few times lightly, "Mom? Are you okay?"

She doesn't answer, and now the light sniffle is turning to gut-wrenching sobs. "Mom! What's going on? Can you open the door, please?"

More crying. No answer.

I don't necessarily believe in clairvoyance or other extra-sensory perceptions, although Ms. Theo did sucker me —and by me, I mean my mom— out of quite a few dollars with her commercials promising details of my future. Give me a break. I was nine! And *none* of what that swindler said came true.

While I don't believe in fortune tellers, I do believe in my gut. I've had some powerful instincts at different points in my life, and I can tell when something ain't right. And right now? Something ain't fucking right.

My whole body is starting to shake, a cold clenching feeling in the pit of my stomach is taking over my senses, and I feel like I could faint.

I squeeze my eyes shut and try to take a deep breath as I reach a shaky hand down to the knob. It's unlocked.

The slow creak of the metal twisting seems to go on forever while my heart thuds to the beat of a thousand wild horses galloping on a barren mountainside.

Whatever I thought to expect on the other side of this door could not come close to the horror show in front of me.

Blood.

Fucking blood *everywhere*.

Iron flows thickly throughout the room, leaving its festering acrid scent to attach to my nostrils and land in the back of my throat.

"M-mom?! Fuck. Are you okay? What is happening here?"

She is slumped in the corner where the wall and door meet and staring blankly at the wastebasket that is overflowing with several filled pads.

"I thought it would be okay, Lola. I really did..." she whispers meekly.

"What would be okay? What's wrong with you?" the words are hard to get out. The lump that resided in my throat has now firmly lodged itself in my chest. I can't breathe. I can't think. What do I *do*?

My knees hit the floor hard, and I gather my mom in my arms as she sobs into the crook of my neck.

She has always been larger than life to me. My hero. The one I look up to. Who kisses my boo-boos, sings silly songs with me, rubs my tummy when I feel sick, and always knows what to do. She's my rock. And my rock is turning to fucking ash in front of my eyes.

I softly rock us back and forth and smooth some of the damp hair off of her forehead, "Shh, it's okay, Mom. I've got you."

Her sobs slow to a devastating whimper with accompanying wet sniffles. I continue to rock us and whisper soothing words until the room falls silent.

Mom lifts her swollen, saturated eyes to mine, and I know her next words are going to crush my fucking soul.

"Oh baby, I'm so sorry," she takes a deep, stuttering breath before continuing, "I thought it was under control and could be taken care of without making a big fuss. I did the tests. I went to the appointments. I took the pills."

"Mom, please tell me what that means." I plead I can't follow her rambling right now. I need her to spell it out for me and be totally clear as to what is happening.

She pulls back from me and snaps her spine straight. She reaches her hand to cup the right side of my face, gently stroking the tears away with her thumb.

She continues to stare with eyes filled with love and turmoil while my gaze resembles a frantic metronome bouncing back and forth between each of her eyes.

"Baby... I have cancer."

Chapter 35

Have you ever felt like you were frozen in a room while everyone and everything around you is moving at hyper speed? That's how I've felt for the last five days since I found Mom huddled in the bathroom, covered in her own blood.

The fog descended, and I've just been... existing. My dad came in, apparently he was in the know of what was going on. I couldn't even find it within myself to be angry at him. I'm glad my mom had at least some support.

I'm still struggling with why she didn't tell me, though. Doesn't she trust me? Couldn't I have been a pillar for her to lean on?

We tried to enjoy our Christmas, but it was very morose around here. I'm not the only one who couldn't find the merriment in the midst of the annihilation of our lives.

Red-rimmed, sullen eyes peered back at me whenever I could actually muster the courage to make eye contact with either of them.

Yesterday, I finally got the nerve to ask the hard-hitting questions. I get my medical knowledge from prime-time TV shows, but I understand enough to know this is very serious.

Words like 'metastasized,' 'stage four,' 'radical hysterectomy,' 'quality of life', and 'end of life plans' have floated in the atmosphere and crashed around the room like a ton of cinder blocks.

What the *fuck*.

The cancer started in her colon. She was unaware anything was wrong until she was having intense cramping and an abnormal amount of bleeding during what she just assumed was a heavy flow month. After several months of dealing with this, she finally made a gynecology appointment.

From there, things went pretty fast. A lot of testing and labs, meetings with doctors of different specialties. One of these appointments was when I had dropped her off for a few hours to get what I know now to be a colonoscopy.

From what the doctors have said, it's fairly common for colorectal cancers to spread to other parts of the body before detection.

As if the 'C' word isn't terrifying enough, apparently, it can also creep undetected through your body like a murdering piece of shit thief lurking in the night. Waiting for you to get cozy and vulnerable in bed before jumping out and stabbing you through the fucking chest to take all your valuables and leave you dying a slow painful death on the shitty carpet with several stubborn recurrent stains that you swore you would replace but never got around to.

That's what life comes down to, I suppose. Everything seems fine and dandy until one day, you find yourself bleeding out, alone, staring at a reminder of all the things you said you would do and never did. I guess we all face down our failures and procrastinations at some point.

I feel so helpless. I want to take it away from her. My mom is the least deserving of something so horrific.

Why couldn't this happen to me instead? I'm the broken one.

I'm the one who already has dark thoughts. I'm the one who lies every time someone sees through the chink in my armor and tries to see what I really am.

It should be me, not her.

* * *

One of the things I've always loved about this run-down shit hole we call home is the roof peak that is directly outside my bedroom window. I've spent many sleepless nights on its surface, gazing at the sky.

On a clear night, Ursa Major is out in her full glory. Seven of the most brilliant stars in the sky congregating just for me. To give me peace. To give me hope. To lead me home.

Some people fear the dark. The unknown. The inky skyline with spine-chilling depth that seems to inexplicably call out and lure victims to its expansive void like sirens to a sailor. Content to live in a predictable, safe bubble.

Not me.

I welcome the abyss. The deep, celestial blanket covering the entire horizon, sprinkled with luminous globes, flashes brilliantly against an ominous backdrop of everlasting darkness.

Like I said, broken.

As I lie here in the crisp winter conditions, arms tucked behind my head and gaze fixed on that broad, dazzling panorama, my mind flits through random memories.

Charlotte– Age Four

I giggle as I burrow deep in the pile of crisp leaves. This is the perfect hiding spot. She'll never find me.

"Where, oh, where could my sweet girl be?" Momma questions.

I slap my hands tightly over my mouth to try and prevent any noises from escaping. My shoulders shake lightly with restrained laughter, sending the damp fronds cascading around my face...

"Lolaaa... where are you, baby? Momma is lonely out here without you. Won't you come join me?" she calls out.

I knew I would be able to outsmart her. My hiding spot is the best!

"If I can't find my precious Lola, who will help me finish all of this delicious hot chocolate... there's no way I can eat ALL of these mini marshmallows on my own!"

Hot chocolate? Mini-marshmallows? Those are my favorites! I start to move and unbury myself.

No, Charlotte, no! Be strong. Momma would NEVER not share her hot chocolate with me... would she? No. Silly girl, no.

I huddle down further. It smells in here. Like dirt and pancakes that have been sitting out for a couple of days and would definitely hurt my tummy if I tried to eat them. No way I'm doing that... again.

Thinking about that turns my tummy, and I slowly roll to my back, a few of the leaves that were covering my body falling to the side and exposing my face to the air. I greedily gulp down some of the freshness.

I hear crunching steps from behind me. I freeze and squeeze my eyes shut. I hold my breath for what feels like forever before the noise stops.

I lay still and silent.

What is THAT?

My eyes fly open as wide as they can go as terror takes over my whole body.

I can feel something slinking across the exposed skin of my ankle.

It's a snake! A rat! A worm! A glob of flesh-eating spiders!

My teeth meet the tender flesh of my lower lip and sink in. I swallow the scream in my throat.

Oh my God! Oh my God! Gross, get off, get off, GET OFF!

I attempt a stealth move of my right foot to cross over my leg and brush it off with my shoe.

Please let that work. What if the creature burrows under my skin and takes over my body or eats me from the inside out? Oh God.

My heart is pounding so loud it must be giving away my position.

I feel the sweat beading at my brow, threatening to fall and leave a trail of salty grossness.

Somehow over the intense sound of my rapid heart beating against my ribs, begging to be let out and run like hell, I hear a very cringy slurp.

A smacking of lips sounds very close behind me.

"Mmm, that was probably my best hot chocolate yet. Too bad I'm all out, and the store won't have any ingredients for at least a year. I wish someone would've shared it with me."

That traitor! She drank it all? Didn't save me none? How dare she!

Before I can convince my body otherwise, I fling into a sitting position, sending the damp, dirty leaves sailing in all directions.

I whip my head to look over my shoulders at the confectioning Judas. I narrow my eyes on her, giving my very best glare.

She smiles sweetly at me, "Oh Lola, there you are, honey. I was calling your name over and over. I was hoping you would help me finish my scrumptious drink, but..." she tips the mug upside down.

I watch in horror as the last – mostly melted – mini marshmallow slides, ever so slowly, down the side and lingers on the lip of the mug for one whole Mississippi before dropping down to the earth.

My nostrils flare with anger. I fist my hands and climb to my feet, propping my fists firmly on my hips.

Momma leans close to my face and blows a hard puff of air across my forehead.

I blink back in surprise, and before I can respond, she throws the mug off to the side of the pile and dives at me. She wraps her arms around me as we roll together, and I land on top of her.

I'm trying to stay mad, but laughter bursts out of me like an overfilled balloon.

She cups my face and coos, "There she is."

I smile back at her and wrap my cold, dirty, moist fingers around her bony wrists.

"Oh! You know what, baby? I just remembered, there's a present for you sitting beside my chair on the porch. Do you want to go check it out?"

I show her all my teeth with my wide smile and nod my head excitedly.

She gently slides her warm hand across my cheek and tilts my chin in the direction of the porch.

My eyes light in pure joy as I see the curl of steam fighting with the cool atmosphere and fading into the air coming from another mug. One that I hope on my whole Barbie collection contains more of my favorite delicious cocoa beverage with a plethora of mini marshmallows atop it like little saccharine clouds.

"I want you to listen up and listen good, Lola. I will never let you go without. I will never forget about you. You are the North Star in my sky, baby. Without you, I would be lost. My cocoa is your cocoa, always. No matter what, I will always find you, and I will always take care of you. You understand?" her soft voice carries over the brisk breeze passing between us and settles deep in my soul.

"I understand, Momma," I respond shyly.

And I do understand, now and forever, that Momma will always take care of me.

"Got room for one more out there, Charlie-Bear?" Dad's voice brings me out of the video rolling through my mind's eye.

I don't respond, but I scoot my hips a little to the left, giving just enough space for him to crawl out and sit beside me without the threat of rolling off and pulling a Humpty Dumpty.

"Do you want to talk about it?" he questions.

I let out a long, thoughtful breath. Do I want to talk about it? What is there to talk about? My mom has cancer. She's going to die. She's already decided against the additional treatments offered to her. She's given up, so what is there to talk about?

I shake my head.

Life, as we both know it, will never be the same again. I snuggle up close to him and rest my head on his lap like I did when I was a child as a tear blazes a hot trail against my temple.

I wish I could go back to that time. When my mom was healthy and not dying. When we were happy as a family. When my parents loved each other. When things made sense. When I felt safe. When the world wasn't constantly trying to eviscerate my fucking life.

When I had hope.

Chapter 36

I don't want to go back to school. What's the fucking point? I don't have it in me to fake anything with anyone right now.

Mom begged me to go, and that's the only reason I'm sitting in this classroom listening to Mr. Vale drone on and on about the importance of Macroeconomics in today's society.

You know what's important, Mr. Vale?

Fucking nothing.

We are all just going to die anyway. By our own hand, someone else's, or some Godforsaken disease.

I let my focus roam to the big picture window boasting a view of the highway with a large snow-capped mountain in the background. *How many bears live on that mountain? I wonder how many bear attacks are actually successful in fatality every year?*

Would getting mauled to death by a bear suck ass? For sure. But maybe it's a preferable death to, let's say, burning or drowning.

Which would be more painful in an attack between a bear and a shark?

Are there any sharks in the waters surrounding Alaska? Surely there has to be.

My internal deep dive into animal attacks is interrupted by a tap on my shoulder. I boredly look behind me and see one of the girls that hang out with Jason and Jade's crew. I think her name is Aurelia.

I've seen her throughout the year in this class, but we've never spoken. She keeps to herself, sitting in the back row with her headphones hugging tightly to her flaming auburn locks. Mr. Vale and the rest of our classmates seem to ignore her existence. She appears comfortable with being insignificant.

She's cute in an innocently Gothy sort of way. Like a baby Lucifer before his jealous rage sent him falling from the heavens.

She has burnt umber freckles dotting a vast majority of visible skin. Her pale complexion is reminiscent of the fur on an Arctic Fox.

I cock an eyebrow at her, questioning.

"Um, Charlotte? A-are you..." she stutters and lets out a nervous cough. "Are you okay?" her soft, kind, unsure sky-blue eyes meet mine.

I tilt my head slightly to the side and narrow my eyes, studying her. "Why do you fucking care, freak?" I bite back at her kindness. Fuck her. She's probably pretending to be concerned so she can gather information on me to take back to her Dark Mommy Overlord. *Nope, not happening, Elvira.*

She flinches as if I've struck her, and I guess, in a way, I have. She shrinks into herself as much as she can. Tucking her fists into the sleeves of her oversized sweater and slides down further in her chair.

"I–I was just asking because you don't look like yourself. You seem really upset. I just t-think Jason isn't... worth it." her voice decreases even further, making me have to lean in her direction and strain to hear her.

I twist my whole body to face her and smash my palm down hard on the top of her desk, making her yelp and jolt in surprise.

"You think that cheating bastard is the cause of this?" I swipe my hand up and down my body to indicate my appearance, "Fuck Jason. This has nothing to do with him." Alright, that's not entirely true. But he is a very small part of my current state of mind. *Very* small.

Aurelia gently shrugs one shoulder, still not meeting my eyes, and it's pissing me off. If she's going to talk about shit she has no business being involved in, then the least she could do is look me in the fucking eyes.

I curl my lip, ready to unleash more vitriol at her. I snarl, "You think you're invisible? Honey, I've seen you follow Jade around like a fucking dog. Begging for scraps of attention. Copying her look, trying to carry yourself with the same arrogance. Did you actually think if you looked and acted like her, Jason would look at you twice?" I cruelly laugh at her; I see the tears start to escape her clenched eyes, but I can't stop now. I knew I had seen that lovesick look in her eyes before. She has a thing for Jason.

I tip my head back towards the water-stained tiles on the ceiling and let out a deep throaty laugh. "Oh, sweetie, you did, didn't you? That's hilariously sad," bringing my razor-sharp stare back to hers, I hiss at her, "You are a fucking joke, Aurelia. At least Jade is original and confident, even if she is a horrid skank. You? You are *nothing.* Pathetic. You will always be a loser. You could kill yourself today, and no one would even notice."

She sucks in a harsh breath and pushes back from the desk, grabbing her backpack off the floor. In her haste to get away, her foot snags on the metal leg of the desk, and she falls forward; the audible sound of her knee smashing against the hard tile perforates the now-silent classroom.

A few muffled laughs sound around the space, bouncing off the walls like an echo chamber.

I slowly move to a standing position and walk over to her. I gently bump her foot with mine, and she recoils, bringing her leg up to her body in a fetal position.

I look over her shaking frame and bend down to a crouch beside her. Reaching my hand out, I gently part her cherry tresses to see her heat-bloomed, tear-stained cheeks.

She is sobbing silently and refusing to open her eyes. I softly run the backside of my index finger against the apple of her cheek as I lean down so close that my lips skim the edge of her ear, "You might be insignificant as yourself, but you are less than *nothing* as someone else."

"Charlotte Johnson! Get the hell out of my classroom. *Now!*" Mr. Vale sneers at me.

Fuck her, fuck him, and fuck this place.

I stand and grab my binder, tucking my pens away before replying with sheer boredom, "Gladly."

I let the heavy wooden door slam behind me, and I stomp to my locker to put my shit away. I need to get out of here.

As I lock the combination and get ready to walk down the hall, *his* scent reaches my senses. No. I cannot deal with this right now.

"Charlotte?" Jason calls from behind me with all the uncertainty his lying, scumbag ass should have.

I close my eyes and let out a long breath. I don't want to talk to him. What is there to say? I can't handle this right now. I need to leave. Fuck him for thinking he can talk to me.

Shaking my head rapidly, I lift my right hand and flip him off as I start to walk away, never looking at him, "Nope, not today, Satan. Go fuck yourself!"

I don't stop until I reach the middle of the parking lot. I look around, feeling lost. My heart is thundering in my chest, and the whomping in my ears is deafening.

I lean against the closest car to me. Closing my eyes and bouncing my head backwards off the door frame.

I was so caught up in my thoughts that I didn't recognize the sleek gray sports car I'd perched on until I heard the owner's recognizable gravelly voice dripping with sleaze.

"Well, Hell's bells. What did I do right in a past life to have the one and only Charlie Johnson land her fine ass on my sweet ride?"

I stare at him blankly, in no mood for his bullshit. I push off the car and jut out my hip while slapping my hand on it, eyeing him critically up and down.

Erick Poole.

River View High's resident bad boy. Known for his flashy lifestyle –hence the car– and number of notches on his bedpost. I've heard more than a few of those notches have happened at the same time.

Erick also happens to be the school's resident drug dealer.

You want it? He can get it... for a price.

My shoulders slump as the weight of the day starts closing in on me. I don't have anything left to give.

"Erick, can we just not today? Please."

He strides over to me, encroaching on my space, backing me up until I'm pressed against the door once again. I gasp, my eyes widening in consternation.

He snakes his hand up my hip, skimming the side of my breast as he continues upward. As his hand finds my shoulder, he squeezes gently before wrapping it around my neck. His grip snug but not crushing. I could get away if I really tried.

Leaning forward, he inhales deeply while running his nose up the side of my neck.

"Tell me what you need, beautiful," he whispers, hot breath sliding against my skin while his lips trail over my pulse point.

My eyes flutter shut as I take a shaky breath, " I need not to feel anymore."

Still with a firm grip against my neck with his left hand, his right hand goes into his jeans pocket and comes back out again, making his way slowly back up my body. He keeps the back of his hand touching me at all times, brushing against all of my sensitive areas.

"You want me to take it all away, baby?" he breathes the words into my mouth with his lips ever so slightly brushing mine.

Eyes still closed, I nod my head.

"Say it." he quietly demands while grinding his hardness against me.

"Please," I whisper against his lips.

"Please, what?" he asks smugly.

I gulp, both knowing and not knowing what I'm asking for.

"Please make it all go away, Erick," I beg.

A smirk makes its way across his mouth. "Open." His tongue lashes my lower lip. I obey his command and open for him; his tongue immediately invades my mouth.

I feel the tablet enter, promptly falling apart as a bitter, sharp taste fills the space.

"Swallow," Erick demands. And I do.

The acrid taste dissipates, and I open my eyes to see Erick's hooded ones gliding lazily along my curves. Curves that he seems to still be pleased with beyond the adornment of Bobos currently wrapping my body.

I don't want to ask, but I have to know. "What do I owe you?" I know he didn't do this out of the goodness of his heart. Erick is a businessman, and there's always a cost to doing business.

My head is beginning to feel a bit cloudy. The clouds settle across my consciousness with a lightness I wasn't expecting. It feels odd... but better... good even.

So good that instead of cringing away when I feel Erick slide his hands into the waistband of my sweats, I tilt my hips towards him.

"That's a good girl." he grits out as his rough fingers find my slit, and he shoves them inside me without any warm-up.

I don't even feel the pain. I don't feel anything as I let him extract his payment.

Chapter 37

"Fuck, I love this filthy mouth of yours. Open wide, baby." Erick's rough hands grip my head and force it backward, tilting my face up towards him as he thrusts into his own hand with a punishing force until he comes into my mouth.

He latches onto my chin, pinching together with sinister energy pouring out of him, "That's it, you dirty whore. Show me your tongue."

I open wider and stick my tongue out as his salty thickness slides down, leaking out of the corners of my mouth. He laps up the excess with his thumb and sticks it in my mouth, "Suck."

After I swallow down the rest of him, my reward comes. My eyes are alight with excitement as he slips the baggie out of his pocket and removes a tablet, and places it on my tongue. I greedily swallow it down dry, not even tasting the bitterness anymore.

The cost of not feeling has gone up over the last few weeks. He doesn't ask for money. He doesn't want for cash; he wants me in the most degrading of ways, and yet I can't bring myself to care. Most of the time, I pay up on my knees. Occasionally if he's feeling generous, he will only require my hands.

I still have no idea what he actually gives me. Part of me is afraid to know. If I stay ignorant, I can pretend it's just your everyday over-the-counter pain reliever.

And it does. Relieve my pain, that is. I just wish I could figure out how to make it last longer.

Erick and I have worked out a system. I come to him, and he asks, "How bad?" and I respond in a multitude of ways, from "I want to be numb" to "Take me to fucking outer space."

The pills differ in color and size, but always the taste stays the same. The pungently bitter pellet starts melting against my tongue, coating it in a numbing fuzz as I force it down my throat.

Erick tucks himself away as he stares down at me, used and broken at his feet. He reaches down and gives a quick sharp slap to my left cheek, "You make a good fucking whore, Charlie. Who knew?" a cruel huff of laughter leaves his body as his eyes dismiss me.

Falling into the comfortable place of not feeling, I stare up at him with blank, unfeeling eyes. He shakes his head at my lack of response and turns around, stalking off in the direction of the door, a resounding click signaling his exit.

Lightness washes over me as I lay flat on the barely carpeted floor of this empty classroom. My eyes jump around without focus on the pocked ceiling tiles, finding a focal point in the blinking red light of the smoke detector built into the rusting ballast surrounding the fluorescent bulbs.

The light grows in size, a mini sun, and I bask in its warmth. I can feel it covering my body, the steady hum of the heating unit like waves beating against a sandy shoreline. The screeching of the water pipes turns to winged beasts circling the sky above, waiting for their opportunity to swoop down and capture their prey.

My head lolls back and forth as I try and fail to shoo them away with the concrete bricks my arms have become.

I chuckle to myself as I somehow fail to scare away the imaginary creatures.

The sun bursts into a supernova; my eyes burn with the intensity. I wait to be engulfed by the flames. And wait. And wait.

"Motherfucker." a gruff voice sounds in the direction of the door.

Weightless. I am weightless, and it feels Ah-fucking-mazing. Floating in space, tumbling away from the shrapnel of the detonated supernova.

" What've you done, Little Bit?" the voice whispers. There's heavy emotion in the words. Too much emotion.

I continue my exploration of the ethereal expanse, following the radiant illumination of stars around me. Glowing brightly and fading to blackness, calling me forth, "Welcome, Charlie. Stay a while."

The ghost-like hands reach down to tuck my unruly locks behind my ears.

"Come back to me, sweet girl."

My lids flutter open, and a resplendent figure cast in a pure white gleam with glowing verdant orbs captures my breath straight from my chest.

I reach my hands to the figure, unbothered by the possibility I may perish at the first touch. I need it to breathe life back into my deflated lungs.

"Give it back, my divine angel," I beg.

His voice cracks through the otherwise quiet space, encapsulating bolts being thrown from the heavens, "Give what back, baby girl?"

"The breath you stole from me." my hands beg for something to grab onto. "I need you." my fingers thread through his soft strands. "I'll die without it." I intertwine my fingers at the base of his neck and tug him down towards me. "Please, angel, give me life. Today I want to live. I want you."

In the shadows of the room, my angel is a burst of light. Emeralds shine down on me from above. I want to live in his gaze forever. His words are garbled transmissions, another language I have yet to learn.

Heat pulsates off him in waves. I luxuriate in it. I want that heat all over me, inside me. Filling me to the point of internal detonation, my own supernova.

"Please, angel."

His lips are within an ace of mine. I can feel his life force. I need more.

"Please."

Warmth cups my face on both sides. An inferno of touch collides with my forehead. My angel finally speaks, "I wanna give you everything, Little Bit. I wanna reach into the heavens to pluck your beloved stars from the sky. I wanna fix everything that feels wrong and broken. I wanna protect you from ever feelin' hurt again. I wanna bury myself so deep inside you that our souls interlock and cannot separate again. I want you, sweetheart— body, mind, and soul. I want you to be mine. But I won't settle for anything less than all of you. Can you give me all of you, darlin'?"

I don't speak. The seraph has stolen my voice, locked it away in an unbreakable box, tucked in a vault inside of a mountain, buried under several feet of dense snow and ice.

He ignores my silence and continues, "I wanna love you, baby. Can you let me do that? Can you open your heart to me and let me see all of you?"

Could I give him what he's asking for?

No. I can't. I don't even know what it means to be that vulnerable and open with someone. I have nothing. I'm poison. I will kill this embodiment of divinity with my toxicity.

The unholy filth inside me will saturate his veins until the light inside is extinguished, turning it into a deep, dark abyss to match the blackness inside me.

A warm burst of mint passes over my face as he lets out a deep, heart breaking sigh.

"I didn't think so. One day, Little Bit. One day."

Chapter 38

3 Months Before Graduation 2006

Eighteen. Officially an adult.

I've been an adult for a week now, and I feel no different. No immediate handbook for life magically appeared on my dresser. I don't have everything figured out all of a sudden. What a fucking joke.

The last few weeks have been filled with numerous doctor visits and talks of treatments – spoiler alert, Mom doesn't want any because of how slim the chance is at this point, and she 'just wants to spend as much time with me as she can' – exams at school that I have barely passed, missing the fuck out of Savvy.

I can't bring myself to confess what's happening in my life to her right now. I've only been able to hide my actions from her because she's been at the University of Central Florida for the last six weeks. Due to her athletic scholarship for cheer she's been able to enter a high school completion program with UCF.

My bestie is living her best life, touring campus, partying, making friends, and making memories. All the things a fresh adult should be doing. I don't want to bring her down.

I've been trying my best to put on a brave facade for Mom. She knows something's up, but she's got so much going on that she hasn't pressed the issue.

Savvy's mom has been over daily, goddamn saint of a woman that Mary Mitchell. She has designated herself as in charge of taking care of Mom. God knows we would both have starved at this point without her casseroles. I hate that I've put her in an awkward position, but I begged her not to tell Savs and ruin her trip. She begrudgingly agreed.

Yesterday almost fucking killed me. Mom asked me to accompany her to Weston Funeral Home. We got to peruse the plethora of final resting place options available there. I learned there are three main types of caskets– Metal, Wood, and Fiberglass. Metal is the preference of most as it comes in a variety of colors and even has linen-lined drawers, so your useless fucking tchotchkes can go to the afterlife with you!

The funeral director walked over to us, hand outstretched with a few pamphlets. Mom opened the cremation one and elbowed me in the ribs, " Mr. Weston? Am I able to request items to be cremated with?" she asked innocently.

"Of course, Ms. Johnson. What items did you have in mind?" he asked in a soft, kind voice.

"I always thought it would be fun to go out with a bang. So I'm thinking about five pounds of hot pink glitter, ten pounds of movie theater butter popcorn kernels, and handfuls of colored sparklers sprinkled around my body at your leisure. I'm open to other color options if pink isn't specifically available." Mom bit down on her lip, desperately trying to keep a straight face.

Mr. Weston was for sure not amused as he barely contained

his eye roll and said "If you'll excuse me, I need to tend to an urgent matter."

As we watched him walk away at a clipped pace, Mom wheezed out, "Hey Lola, what are caskets made out of?" the deathlike pallor of her face barely attached to the protruding bones of her cheeks. Her dry, chapped lips tried their best to lift in a slightly amused smile.

I smiled brightly at her even though my heart felt like it was being ripped apart with searing hot bear claws. I cocked a brow in her direction, "What are they made out of, Mother?" I questioned, surprising myself with the amount of amusement that I was able to inject into the words.

"MOURNING wood." she quips. She tries to laugh but ends up coughing hard into her white handkerchief. She quickly attempted to get it back in her purse, but I saw the crimson dots that lined the otherwise unblemished fabric.

I pretend I didn't see it. I'm getting good at pretending with her.

* * *

If I twist the bulb, it will work, right? Right. I've seen Momma do it before. It looks easy.

She told me not to touch it because it gets really hot, but if I wait five Mississippi's, it won't be hot anymore. I think.

I reach out and tug the cord from the wall, it takes a lot of strength but it finally gives and comes out. I pulled a little too hard, and the thick metal part flew back and hit me in the shin ow.

I roll my tan corduroy pant leg up to my knee and expose the fresh red spot, highlighting my otherwise unblemished shin; with a frown, I rub my fingers gently over the top of the offending spot while I start my Mississippi count.

One Mississippi. Maybe I should get Momma and have her help me.

Two Mississippi. But she's making dinner, and I'm not supposed to make treats on my own.

Three Mississippi. I can taste the gooey, warm brownie already.

Four Mississippi. It's been long enough, right?

The moment my fingers touch the very much still hot bulb, a shrill scream leaves my body. Pain like I've never felt travels from my fingertips up my arm, and I'm pretty sure my insides are now as partially baked as my Supreme Fudgy Chocolate Chunk Brownie.

Yeah, my guts are definitely liquifying as I sit here in agony. I definitely shoulda waited that extra Mississippi before touching it.

I let out another primal scream.

I've lived a good life these last six years. I hope Momma gives my toys to some other little girl who will cherish them the way I do.

She'll play with the dolls gently, put them in the right outfits, clean their accessories, make sure their shoes match, and they always, always, ALWAYS get their hair washed once a week with Momma's special strawberry serum.

On second thought, no one will take care of them the way I do. They can just go with me in my coffin.

I jump up to grab my Little Mermaid suitcase and begin putting all my dolls in a neat row. I start on the accessories next, and I hear Momma's voice from my doorway, "Lola, what's wrong, baby? Why are you packing?"

"I'm dying, Momma, and no other little girl will love my dolls as much as me, so they are going with me!" I shout frantically at her while still carefully packing.

Momma kneels in front of me and gently places her hands on my wrists, I furrow my brow, she can't slow me down. I have to get these things together. Doesn't she know my time is almost up?!

"Lola?"

"No, Momma, time's almost up. I can feel it. I have to be quick!" Why is she so calm?

"Baby girl, look at me and tell me what's going on, please."

I blow out a big breath and look up into her hazel eyes that look kinda like mine, except mine are darker, like my brownie mix. "Momma, my insides are burning. I'm half-baked already, and time is about up for me. I want my dolls to go in my coffin with me. Do you understand? You told me not to touch the bulb. I counted to four Mississippis and thought it wouldn't be hot anymore. You told me I shouldn't touch it and wait for you if it stopped working, and I shoulda listened to you. You are so smart, and you always know the right thing, and I was bad and didn't listen. I touched the bulb, and it started a fire inside my body, so now I die. All because I didn't want to wait for one more measly Mississippi!"

She sits down beside me and gathers my withering body into her arms, and begins rocking me back and forth. I feel myself getting sleepy. This must be it. At least I can die in my momma's arms. I snuggle my head into her shoulder and breathe her flowery scent in.

She pulls my fingers to her mouth and places soft kisses on each one, it tickles so I can't help but giggle but I keep my eyes squeezed tight because, you know, I'm dying still.

"Momma?" I rasp out with my ever-weakening voice.

She runs her fingers through my hair, "Yes, baby?"

"What do you want to be in your coffin with you when you die?"

She makes a 'hmmm' noise like she does when she's really thinking about something.

"I would want my Hummel figurines, obviously. My leather

jacket from the one and only rock concert I went to. My View–Master, so I don't get bored. My Red Apple roll on chapstick. And the little satin case in my dresser with the baby teeth you've lost so far."

"Ew, Momma, my teeth? I thought you were saving those for when the Tooth Fairy is ready to take them back home with her?"

"Oh no, I made a deal with her that if I get to keep the teeth, she can have all of your daddy's adult teeth when he gets old and needs dentures. She never gets big people's teeth and seemed very excited by the trade, so now, all your little chompers are MINE!" she growls and turns her hand into a claw as she tickles my sides until I beg her to stop and threaten to pee my pants.

As I struggle to breathe through my laughter, I realize my insides aren't burning anymore. Maybe I'm not dying after all. Momma makes everything better.

Chapter 39

Should I feel guilty for taking some of Mom's pain pills that I found in the bathroom? Probably.

Is that stopping me from doing it? Definitely not.

She hardly even takes them. She doesn't like the way they make her feel numb and disconnected from everything. She wants to be present and alert. All the things that I don't, so I take them.

I place two round, beige tablets on my tongue and force them dry down my throat. I should probably eat today. It's becoming harder and harder to remember to do that.

My once curvy body has slimmed down to the point of protruding hip bones and exposed ribs. My normal clothes sag in all the wrong places. I've covered up the weight loss with my consistent wardrobe of Bobo's.

Everyone attributes my gaunt face, darkened eyes, and lack of effort in my appearance to my mom's 'situation'.

I've turned into a bit of a social pariah at school. Between my breakup with Jason, avoidance of Zach, outburst at Aurelia,

Savvy's absence, and being seen periodically with Erick, people give me a wide berth, and I'm glad for it.

My reprieve from questions ends tomorrow when Savs comes back from Florida. I'm happy she's coming home because I miss her. I also dread her coming home because she's going to lose her fucking mind when she sees me and hears who I've been spending my time with.

A song sounds out from my TV as the DVD inside repeats the title menu over and over, something about today being a perfect day. Before I hit play on Elle Woods for a fifth time this week, I need some sustenance. I flop off my bed sideways, standing straight up I can feel the warm numbness descend over the rest of my body, wrapping me tight like a prickly cocoon.

I open my door slowly, mindful of any creaks in case Mom is sleeping. I tip my head out of the opening, tilting my ear down the hall towards the living room. I can hear hushed whispers.

Curious, I step lightly down the hall, careful to miss the board I know will give me away.

My mom's raspy voice carries down the hollow hallway, "Gray called. He wanted to know if he could bring Alexis to Charlotte's graduation. Apparently, he proposed to her a few weeks ago and wants her to be a part of such an important family day." Dad got engaged? I knew he had a girlfriend, but I didn't think they were that serious. What the fuck. Why wouldn't he tell me?

I hear a sarcastic snort, "It wasn't enough for that whore to fuck my husband and break up my family. Now she wants to be included in MY daughter's special day? I don't fucking think so. You know, Mary, I've done everything I can to keep our family together and not let his affair tear us apart. Obviously, our marriage was over, but I kept things civil for Charlotte's sake. She didn't need to lose two parents because Gray couldn't keep his dick in his pants. So even though it was the most painful thing I've ever had to do, I put on a smile and told our daughter a version of the truth that wouldn't make her hate her father. And how does he repay me? By marrying the homewrecker and trying to replace me as her mother when I'm about to fucking die!" she starts coughing on her shout.

I'm frozen in the hallway. Eyes unblinking. Chest not inflating with breath. Synapses misfire throughout my brain, trying to make sense of what I just heard.

That can't be right. They split because they grew apart. That's what they told me.

But... Dad cheated? They lied to me? He's marrying his mistress?

No. *No.* This can't be real.

I turn and flee back to my room, closing the door with the slightest snick. I rush to my dresser, frantically pushing undergarments out of the way until my fingers find the baggie tucked away in the back. I take a deep breath and tip two tablets into my palm and pop them in my mouth.

I grab my phone and climb back into bed. I snuggle deep under the covers and unlock my phone screen. The light immediately fills the small space, and I wince at its brightness. I close my eyes briefly, debating my next move.

There's no coming back from this if I do it. Nothing will be the same again.

I take a deep breath and crack each knuckle before shaking my head loose. I nod in affirmation, "Fuck it." I say aloud as I cross the line I swore I never would.

Me: I want to meet him.

Erick: Haha. I have to ask, are you sure? He's a whole new beast, baby.

Erick: You think I'm a villain? His name may be Priest, but he's anything but saintly. He's a true monster, and once he gets a hold of you, he'll never let go.

Me: Just set it up.

Fuck. What am I doing? I don't even recognize myself anymore. I don't recognize anyone. Everything is a fucking lie. I'm already dead, so why not walk into Hell? Bring on the monsters.

Erick: Friday 10 pm. I'll pick you up. Wear something pretty for us. Leave the panties at home.

Chapter 40

1 Month Before Graduation 2006

I involuntarily wince as I step into the shower. My battered body is so tired. I turn the knob all the way left and stand in silence as the glacial streams pelting my skin turn to daggers dipped in hellfire.

Staring down at my skin, I find myself wishing it would melt right off the bones. No inch of it is unsullied. There's no loofah strong enough to scrub away the depravity inked into my flesh. No water hot enough to cleanse my sins away. Even if I could manage to feel clean in my skin, my memories are always there to replay my darkest moments like a deranged carousel, round and round, over and over.

I sink to my knees as memories assault me.

"Boys, this is a fucking fresh one. Check out this tight pussy." Hands grip my body all over. I can hear grunts, taunts, dirty and vile things being spoken about me. My eyes won't open, no matter how hard I try, they are cemented shut.

But I can feel.

I feel as the first man takes me. I feel as fingers force their way into my mouth.

I feel the crushing grip around my windpipe. I feel the searing pain of hair gripped in a tight fist.

I feel the forceful thrusts rocking my body up and down. I feel the dank burst of breath in my ear as his tight, angry words reach me. "Yeah, you fucking love this, don't you, you filthy slut?"

I feel the sting as a palm cracks across my cheek. "She fucking likes it rough, boys; give her what she wants." I feel the clothes being torn from my body. "I'm going to enjoy this far more than you will, you pathetic bitch."

I feel the scream trapped in my throat as a red-hot pain flows through my breasts with the crushing force twisting them. I feel my body being flipped with ease like I'm nothing more than a rag doll.

I feel the rugged hands that grip my ass cheeks and force them apart. I feel my soul leave my body as some nameless, faceless monster takes what was not freely given.

Sobs torment my body as I rock back and forth, my red-tinged arms wrapped tightly around my knees.

A pounding sounds on the door but I'm too lost in my own torment. I can't respond. All I can hear are the repeated sounds of my torture. All I can feel are the hands that mean me harm.

I want to die.

I want to die.

I want to *die.*

Arms band around me tightly from behind.

Please let me fucking die.

Her broken words reach my ears, "Please, Charls. Tell me what's wrong. What happened to you? I don't want you to go. I need you. What can I do? What do you need? Please Charlie. Please let me help you," she implores into my back.

I didn't realize I was begging out loud.

I latch onto Savvy's sopping sleeve-covered arm and twist to look into her horror-stricken face as she takes in the damage to my body. "Savs.." I croak "I can't do it anymore. Please..."

Tears begin to stream down her face, she cups my cheeks searching my eyes for answers that I can't bring myself to give her.

"I'm here. I'm here. I'm here." she chants as she brings our foreheads together.

She's here, but I'm not. I'm so far away and I don't want to come back.

* * *

Savvy didn't leave my side for the rest of the day. We cuddled in silence in my bed. She didn't ask any more questions, and I'm thankful for that. I'm not ready to talk about it.

"Girls, are you still awake?" Mary asks from the barely open crack in my bedroom door.

"Yeah Mom, what's up?" Savvy responds.

"I'm going to head home, Ellie is sleeping..." she pauses, I can hear the hesitation in her voice. I wait to see if she'll continue.

"Charlie, you really need to speak to your father. Your mom needs more constant care and I can't make these decisions for your family. Please, sweetheart, I know you are angry, but please set that aside for your mom's sake and answer his calls."

Is she serious? That man deserves nothing from me. Mom and Mary knew I overheard their conversation a few weeks ago and Mom must've given Dad the heads up because he's been blowing up my phone ever since. Fuck him.

I dismiss her and roll over to face the wall.

I hear her exhausted sigh before she pulls the door to just barely crack open.

Why is everyone insistent on me talking to my dad? I know exactly how that conversation will go. He will feed me some bullshit about not meaning to hurt Mom, you can't help how you feel, love is love. You know the utter pathetic responses cheaters tend to give to avoid accountability.

He will fucking mansplain the destruction of our family and try to twist it into him being the victim for just following his heart.

Yeah, spare me.

A buzzing shakes me out of my patricidal thoughts.

New Group Chat: Savvy, Charlie, Lisa, Jenny

Lisa: OMFG Charlie have you heard about Jason????

Jenny: Girl... how fucking dare he parade that skeeze around like she didn't homewreck your life!

Lisa: A couple of the girls were at The Coffee Hut earlier and saw them cuddled up, and you know Kels is a nosy bitch, right? So she was eavesdropping and overheard them talking about a possible engagement!

Jenny: WTF! They are 17! He literally had his dick in Charlie like a couple months ago, now he's ready to marry someone else?!

Lisa: Right?!

Jesus Christ. I can't even process this information.

If he actually loved me, there's no way he could be getting this serious with someone else so soon, right? Just friends my fucking ass.

He wouldn't have been able to move on so quickly and

pretend like it didn't happen, and it didn't mean anything.

My heart hurts. I still love him. I don't know why I do, but I do. I wish I could shut it off. Remove him from my heart.

Why is every man in my life so utterly disappointing?

Another buzz alerts me to yet another text from the gossip twins. I honestly don't even know why I'm friends with these girls. They are the type to smile in your face and fuck your boyfriend behind your back. I definitely consider them more Savvy's friends than mine.

I look back at my screen and my blood freezes. I only catch the notification bar for a brief second before the message disappears.

Zach: Hey there Little Bit... I wa...

My heart is palpitating at top speed like it was making the last lap around the track at the Daytona 500. Fuck me. I shouldn't add yet another complication right now. I feel a kinship with Zach that scares me.

I was intensely drawn to him from day one. Yes, he's objectively attractive, but it's more than that. He can read me like a book. An open book. A book for beginners. I don't think I could lie to him if my life depended on it. He would see right through me.

The kiss we shared, although I know it was wrong at the time, felt so fucking right. Like our souls were intertwining. Like I was coming home.

I fold my lips together and squeeze my phone tightly in my hand, pressing it into my chest.

I have no choice. I'm pulled to this boy in a way I can't begin to understand.

I hold my breath as I swipe the screen open.

Chapter 41

1 Month Before Graduation 2006

Zach: Hey there, Little Bit... I wanted to see if you'd be down to meet up tonight.

Am I down to meet up with him?

I bite down on my cheek as I start to weigh the pros and cons of doing this.

On one hand, I am a fucking mess, and I shouldn't be dragging anyone else down into my bullshit.

On the other hand, I deserve one good thing going on in my life right now.

Fuck it.

Me: Where and when?

Zach: Sky Ridge. Now.

I lock my phone screen and turn my head as softly as I can to peek over at Savvy. I stifle a giggle as I see her mouth hanging wide open while snores leave her in soft little puffs. Such a mouth breather.

My stealth skills are being put to the test as I shimmy down the bed, cursing myself for putting it up against the wall to give more floor space. The satin sheets show me favor with their silence, not giving my position away.

And immediately take a payment out of my ass by letting it slip right off of the edge and collapsing into a puddle on the floor. *Ouch.*

I quickly grab my sweats and tug them over my boyshorts, wincing at the pull on my already sore muscles. Walking over to my dresser, I pull open the door and stick my hand to the familiar location at the back, ease already spreading through my chest at the feeling I know will soon encapsulate my body.

I look back at Savvy's sleeping form as I reach ever so gently for my keys; I stop all movement and breathing when two of them clack together and sound out like a blaring alarm at a maximum security prison, alerting the guards to an escape attempt. My eyes widen as she twitches. I watch in horror when her foot kicks out from under the blanket. *Come on, Savs, stay the fuck asleep.*

Her soft snore begins again, my lungs begin to burn with the trapped breath and I finally let go.

Thank God Mary didn't close the door all the way.

I carve a path down the hallway, avoiding the loud areas from memory. Barely audible speaking flutters along the walls as I round the corner. The glow of the TV dances along the silhouette of Mom's sleeping body. I watch her chest rising and depleting, with more effort than it should take. I'm light on my feet as I make my way beside her. I bend and place a featherlight kiss along her clammy forehead.

A lump forms in my throat, and I have to fight back the tears that beg to come forth. I gently pull the afghan further up her chest.

"I love you so much, Momma. Please don't leave me." I beg

in a whisper.

* * *

There he is.

Illuminated like some tanned Adonis sitting atop my picnic table.

Goosebumps sprout through my body, tickling my thighs as they rub against the soft cotton of my sweats.

I take a moment to study this boy.

He knows I'm here because my headlights have lit him up like the Christmas tree at Rockefeller Center during the holidays. But he has yet to look up. *Curious.*

My head tilts to the side as I continue studying his form. His very perfect form.

His feet are adorned with his coveted black and gray DVS skate shoes. Tanned and barely-haired calves are partially obscured by the hem of his navy blue athletic shorts. Matching his shorts is a white athletic muscle shirt.

Shiny, thick tree trunks for arms rest heavily on his knees as he leans forward, fingers interlocked and facing the ground.

The sandy tresses I adore seem darker than normal.

My heart is racing. *Calm down, Charlie.*

Crooning melodies float from the speakers, weaving through my body. Something about knocking on Heaven's Door.

I fist the small baggie tightly and thump my hand against my thigh. *Once. Twice. Three times.* I just want to feel good.

I fucking do.

The decision is made as I pop a tablet in my mouth and swish it down with a mostly empty, flat, and very tepid soda left behind from God knows when.

My hands begin to shake as I reach for the keys in the ignition, switch them to OFF, and remove them to rest in their typical place in the free cup holder.

I'm a marionette, numbly moving in the direction my master pulls. One foot in front of the other until I feel the heat of his body.

He still hasn't looked at me. How could I blame him? I've been a complete basket case lately. I don't even recognize myself. *I don't deserve him.*

His head shoots up, and we lock eyes. His normally vibrant ones are dull and reddened, brimming with unshed tears.

Burning tendrils constrict around my heart as I watch this beautiful creature break before me.

I drop to my knees before him, resting my forehead against his twined hands. I can't stand to see the pain staring back at me. *I don't deserve him.*

My hands snake up his calves, and I engulf each one inside my arms, bringing my hands back closer to my chest.

Absentmindedly running my thumb back and forth across his skin, I feel a tight pinch to the back of my head where the hair tie holds my thick tresses in a high pony.

My gaze is forced to meet his tortured one once more. I cringe as I watch a tear leap from his eyes and come crashing down onto the bench seat. This amazingly strong boy. *I don't deserve him.*

A sharp huff stops the tracking of my runaway tear, "Stop fuckin' sayin' that!" he growls at me.

Shocked, I blink rapidly and stutter out, "W-what? Saying what?"

"That you don't deserve me."

Fuck me, I didn't realize I said it aloud.

"But I don't. Zach, if you knew what was good for you, you would run. Far and fast. I am falling deeper and deeper down a hole that I have no idea how to get out of. Every day, my soul dies a little more. I am nothing but a husk of the girl I once was, and I can never be that girl again. You have no idea about the things that I live with every day. No idea of the pain I'm in and the pain I've caused. I'm not worth it." I choke back the emotion that begs to escape, clinging desperately to my own tears that intend to riot at any moment.

A cool mist settles over my bones, and I know it's been enough time. Quick release is right.

My mouth feels like it's been dipped in pop rocks-infused cotton candy. My tongue glides across my front teeth, "I'm not worth anything beyond what my body can offer, and apparently even that is passable if you ask my ex–"

His grip gets tighter on my hair, "I didn't."

"What?" I ask.

"I didn't ask for that fuck-wits opinion, and I don't give a shit what it is. I know what I see. I know what I feel. And I know you're goin' through somethin'. I'd like to help if you'd let me. Because you see, Little Bit, I, too, am fallin' deeper and deeper into a hole I can't get out of," his grip loosens as his hands frame my face, and he tilts my chin further up. "But the difference between us is, I don't wanna come out of the hole. I wanna dig and dig until I unearth every possible treasure. I wanna plant my flag. Stake my claim. I. Want. You."

The riot begins.

My anesthetized body crumbles to the dirt, not feeling any pain from the sharp gravel against my skin.

Warm, dewy arms scoop my body up as if it were lighter than

air.

Zach sits back on the picnic table with my sobbing form gathered tightly against his body, cradled in his arms.

"D–d–don't," I beg. Shaking my head rapidly back and forth.

"Shh, Little Bit, it's okay."

"Please, Zach. I don't want to ruin you. And I will. You are destined for greater things than this. I'm not being cute or humble when I say I don't deserve you. When I say it, it's because I truly mean it. You deserve better than me and what I can give you."

"What can I do?"

I wish I knew. "It's just all so heavy. When does it stop? I feel like I'm constantly being buried under the weight of the world. Just for a little while, can we just pretend? Will you pretend with me?"

"I'll do anything for you, Little Bit."

"Kiss me. Kiss me like we only have tonight."

For all I know, that might be all we'll ever get.

Chapter 42

2 Weeks Until Graduation 2006

It's been two weeks since I met Zach at Sky Ridge, and we've been having daily make-out sessions since. I need the escape that he provides. It's different from pills. His escape never leaves me feeling empty afterward.

We haven't had sex. Not for a lack of trying on my part. His southern gentlemanly side has emerged at the most inconvenient time. He wants to do it right and not on a table in the middle of an open to the public park. Or a car. Or the woods. Or in the grass.

I've propositioned him in all of the above to no avail. The boy's pants might as well be cemented to his body... and I'm trying to drill into them.

Mom is not doing well. She's close to the end, and we all know it. It's been a somber past few months.

I have moments of clarity when I realize I should be spending all my time with her, whether she's conscious or not— most of the time, she's not. I shove that clarity into a deep, dark hole instead opting for blissed-out ignorance.

I'm a horrible daughter. I know it. I just don't know how to handle the fact that my mom– my rock, my hero, my first best friend, the woman who so selflessly hid her own heartache to keep the appearance of happy families– will be ripped from this earth well before her time.

I'm not ready.

So, I do what I do best and deflect, ignore, and numb myself to the point of weightlessness. Nothing matters then. No physical pain. No emotional torment. Just pure nothing, and I love it.

* * *

"Well boys, the new product is finally ready for distribution. Erick, you'll take River View, as usual. Rick, you'll take everything from 12th Street and up. Bennie will scoop up all things south of 8th." Priest divvies out his directions to the runners.

"Yo, Priest, when are we gonna get to test this shit out? Looks like it's got your girl over there flying fucking high." Rick snickers out, locking eyes with me from across the room. That familiar disgust flows through me as I recall his voice from *that* night.

I manage a mumbled, "I'm not his girl."

A sharp slap sounds through the music-filled air, I don't feel the sting, but I do feel the grip of Priest's gorilla paws squeezing the fuck out of my thigh. That's definitely going to bruise.

"You are whatever the fuck I say you are. You got that, Astra?"

The rustling of plastic draws my focus to the stained wooden coffee table. The glass in the center is decorated with various residues of drugs past.

Priest is a sadistic bastard. He thought it'd be funner – for him— to watch me snort the pills.

He didn't ask; he never does; he just grabbed the ridged card and began to line it up.

I got a hand slammed to the throat and a breath-stealing squeeze for the giggle I let out upon being handed the straw.

It was one out of a kid's juice bottle. Short and pink with a tiny figurine of Minnie Mouse on the side.

The familiar grinding on the glass kicks up my heart.

Priest lines four up. There are five of us in the room. He never partakes when people are around. Gotta stay ready at all times, I suppose.

Snorts, sharp inhales, coughs, and throat clears fill the space around us.

This new pill he's developed is a fun ride.

It hits fast and hard; the up lasts for a few hours, and the back end is like a sedation trickling into your veins.

That's the part I enjoy the most. Watching the world shut off like an old TV screen that fades to blackness with a few seconds lag.

The blur before the fade is the peak of the ride for me.

My head lolls to the side against the back of the couch as it settles over me.

"Fuck, man. Yo Priest, this ish is bangin'." Rick sounds out slowly as his ride begins.

A deep inhale and contented sigh comes from Bennie, "Yeah man, there ain't gonna be any problems unloading product for sure. "

"So what does this label mean? What are we calling it?" Erick asks as he toys with the small bag.

I know the label well. I designed it.

It's an image of hellfire burning into the night sky, hellfire so bright and strong that the very stars that hold up the sky come melting down.

AstraMalum.

That's what the bastard decided to name it. An 'homage' to us, apparently. He calls me Astra, apparently my love for the stars is a topic of conversation when I'm laid out. Malum is what I call him. He's the fucking devil—Evil. Enough said.

He turns that evil grin towards me and winks. I try my best to roll my eyes and look away.

"AstraMalum."

Chapter 43

Graduation Day 2006

"It's fucking itchy, and it looks dumb as hell," I complain to Savvy as I straighten the cap and gown for the hundredth time.

"Well, maybe you should've worn more clothes under there," she teases as she picks up the bottom of my gown to reveal my bare legs in only a pair of her cheer shorts.

"You know my body is like a firenado nowadays, and we're all going to be packed together like sardines in the auditorium." I rip my gown out of her hand and smooth it back down. Immediately regretting it because the goddamn wool-covered fiberglass material is clawing at my flesh again. "Besides, Mrs. Beckett is going through 'the change' and is keeping her home at a balmy sixty-five degrees so we get to deal with Mr. Beckett's over-correction of temperature."

I look around for my black flats. There is no sense in dealing with painful footwear when this gown hangs so low that no one can see them anyway.

I spot one on the edge of my reading chair and start to slip it on.

"Okay, that makes sense, I guess, for the ceremony, but what about after? Aren't you going to bring a change of clothes for pictures and whatnot?" she asks.

My hands stop their descent to the underside of the dresser, where I've spotted the other flat, "Savvy, I'm not staying around for all of that. You know my mom's not doing well, and I don't want to stress her out or have her get all those pitying looks people tend to give her when they see her now. It kills me," I choke back a sob, "the only reason I'm walking today is because she asked me to, and I won't deny her this one last–" warm arms band around my middle as my bestie tucks her cheek against my back. "I know, Charlie. It's okay, don't worry about the clothes. We'll walk, get our diplomas, shake some hands, throw some hats, and be out."

"No, Savs, you need to stay. You've got your team, your friends, your mom. I'll leave, but you stay. Got it?" I plead with her.

She nods solemnly, "Got it."

* * *

"Charlotte Belle Johnson." Applause fills the auditorium as I stand. I look back and make eye contact with Mom; she looks so fragile.

Her body is sickly thin, her once full cherubbed face has turned into protruding, sharp cheekbones and a permanent band of black under her watery, bloodshot eyes.

She manages a weak smile and a low wave.

I give her my best attempt at a grin before heading up to the stage. My classmates' faces swim together around the room. Low murmurs sound out around me.

A hushed conversation perks my ears as I pass, "I heard someone saw her giving Erick a blowjob in the parking lot."

"OMG, no way! How the mighty have fallen. From ice queen virgin princess to filthy truck stop whore in no time flat."

I try to ignore the whispers as I pass. What can I say? They are pretty spot on. If Charlotte one year ago saw the Charlotte of today, she'd be in complete disbelief.

I had a rough plan and goal for the trajectory of my life back then.

Finish high school, volunteer at the hospital through the summer, apply for nursing school – somewhere.

Then Jason happened.

I'm not blaming everything on him. I know I made choices too. I'm culpable in the destruction of my existence.

Beyond all boy drama, there's Mom. Never have I pictured a life without her in it.

I overheard her on the phone a few weeks ago, hoping and praying that she would be able to see me graduate. That she wouldn't forgive herself for dying before I hit this 'very big life milestone'. Like I give two fucks about high school.

The only reason I've gone to school this semester is because she begged me to live life 'normally'. Like what the fuck does that even mean?

I've never known a normal.

My brain is broken. I was born defective. One minute I feel great, school is great, friends are great, living is great. Great. Great. *Great.*

Until it's not. I don't get a warning. Just instant deflation.

Some invisible douchebag is out there following me around

and waits until I'm at a point of being content and maybe even a tiny bit happy, then he stabs his little sword right in the 'okay' bubble surrounding me.

As I deflate, I fall further and further to the ground until I'm one with the dirt.

I shake my head loose from the torrent of thoughts and step lightly on the staircase, locking eyes with a smiling Mr. Clarke. He beckons me forward with an outstretched hand.

I look back out to Mom, who is now sobbing into her hoodie sleeves. I can just barely see her eyes over the cuffs. I give her a sweet smile, and as I shake hands with our principal, I see her fall into a coughing fit. Fuck.

His words of congratulations and well wishes go in one ear and out the other, I just want to get her out of here.

I nod my head and offer thanks as I scurry off the stage. Passing by Ms. Thomas, I lean down to whisper, "My mom isn't doing well, and I need to get her home. Can I please return my cap and gown next week? I promise I will."

She gives me a weak smile and pats the top of my hand, "Of course, dear, I'll mark it down for you." I start to walk away. Her voice carries to my back. "And Charlotte?" I stop my forward motion and turn to face her, eyebrows raised in question. "I'm so sorry." I nod sharply once and walk away.

"Oh, Lola, I am so proud of you, baby. Congratulations. Give your momma a hug." Mom reaches out for me with those frail arms. I make sure I gather her up gently. She bruises so easily nowadays and seems to always be in pain.

"Thanks, Momma, I love you. I appreciate you being here." I regret my words as soon as they come out, and I see her smile fall. I didn't mean 'here' like alive. I just meant the ceremony. But lately, anything can turn into talks of her impending demise. There's no way around it. Long gone are the days we joke about her expiration; it's way too real now.

"I'm sor–"

She interrupts my apology with a cold hand to my cheek."Shh, sweet girl. I know what you meant. Now what do you say we get out of here and grab some PizzaGuy? Hm? A little fettuccine with a side of donut holes? Maybe a splash of cheese curds? We could split a Denali Lumberjack pizza!"

Yeah, PizzaGuy has a pretty eclectic menu, and they always keep coloring pages and drawings plastered to the walls. They have barely any open space left. I enjoy looking for my past works. The last time we went, I spotted a masterpiece from age four. I begged them to let me take it, but Mr. PizzaGuy himself basically told me to go fuck myself.

We both know there's no way she's eating much of anything, but it's a good-ish day for both of us, and I don't want to waste our precious time, so I nod excitedly.

Chapter 44

We make it to the parking lot, about fifteen feet from our car, when I hear my name shouted from the crowd behind us. Turning, I see someone I have absolutely no desire to see or speak to, jogging towards me with a big grin on his face like he didn't ruin our whole fucking lives.

"Charlie-bear, congratulations. I am so proud of you. You looked so beautiful and grown up on that stage. I probably took two hundred photos!" he rushes out, partly out of breath from his jog.

The only acknowledgment he gets from me is a stoic face and a raised eyebrow. The tick in his jaw gives away his disappointment with my reaction.

I tip my head in his direction, "Grayson."

He sighs, wringing his hands together as he tries to plead with me, "Charl–"

I look around him, searching the crowd before looking directly into his eyes. A deviant smirk takes over my mouth, "Where's the mistress, Grayson?"

"W-what?" he stutters out, looking between me and my mom in disbelief.

"Charlotte Belle!" Mom admonishes, but I give zero fucks. I wave off her use of my government name.

"The mistress, Grayson. Where is she? Hiding in the shadows somewhere?" I make a big show of peeking around the parking lot with suspicion dripping from my words.

"Recovering from a breast augmentation that you paid for? Inspecting the pool boy's work 'extra close,' if you know what I mean?" I give him a sarcastic wink, "How you get 'em is how you lose 'em, Grayson."

"That's enough, Charlotte. I am your father, and you do not get to speak to me this way. And it's 'Dad' to you, young lady."

I can't help it; I start laughing, "Oh, that's rich coming from you, *Grayson*," I slap my hand to my thigh like it's the funniest damn thing I've ever heard. "You're basically a sperm donor. You chose to move across the country because your side piece and career were more important than being with your actual family. With me." I smack my palm to my chest. "You think you deserve 'Dad' because you call every now and then, send gifts, and fly out for holidays? Fuck you, *Grayson*. Go back to your Stepford existence and leave me alone."

My sperm donor stares in disbelief at me. Mouth agape and unsure what to do next. My mom gasps from behind me, which turns into another coughing fit. I turn and take her gently by the elbow and help her get into the passenger seat before making my way to the driver's side.

Looking at him one last time, still staring at me, bewildered. I shake my head and get in the car.

"Charl–" Mom starts.

"Please, Momma. I don't want to talk about him. Can we please just have the day we planned and not worry about anything else right now? Just me and you. Please?" I beg.

She sighs and nods softly, "Okay baby, me and you. Let's go."

* * *

If I had known this would be the last PizzaGuy outing Mom and I would have together, I would've cherished it more.

If I had known four days later would be the last time we got a slushy together, I would've sipped it more gently.

If I had known when she tucked me in and said goodnight eleven days ago would be the last time I would've asked her to crawl in with me.

If I had known the hug I gave her fourteen days later would be the last one, I would've squeezed her a little tighter.

If I had known the last time I would see life in her eyes would be sixteen days later, I would've memorized every line. Every variation of color. The way her pupils dilated with happiness just looking at me.

If I had known the last time I would see her earthly form would be eighteen days later when we lowered her into the ground, I would've... fuck. What could I have done? Be more prepared?

If I had known.

Chapter 45

There's a fucking bleach spot on my shoe. How does that even happen? It's not like I was cleaning and thought, "Hm, you know what would be a good idea? To wear my nicest, black Vans while I bleach the tub."

When was the last time I even wore these?

I'm brought out of my perplexity by the Pastor's words, "Amelia, or Ellie as those close to her called her, was an irreplaceable part of this community. She always had kind words for those around her. Ellie would volunteer at the local women's shelter yearly, ran several of our clothing drives for the homeless, and put together hygiene kits for those in need out of her own pocket," he pats his stomach, "not to mention she made the best-deviled eggs I've ever had the pleasure of tasting. Sorry Charlene." his gaze lovingly finds his wife off to the left side of the pew as he teases her.

The crowd lets out a soft laugh.

"She will be greatly missed by all who were privileged enough to know her, and I know there will be an Ellie-sized hole in my life that can never be filled. May you all find comfort in the Lord's grace and lean on each other as we carry on her memory. We should all strive to live up to the examples of selflessness and generosity that our Sister Ellie embodied." he pauses to swipe a stray tear away, clearing his throat before continuing. "I'd now like to invite her daughter, Charlotte, up to the pulpit to say a few words," he extends his hand in my direction, "Dear?"

I close my eyes and take a deep breath. My hands are clammy and stick to the notebook paper on which my long-winded speech is written.

I take turns rubbing each hand over the material of my black skater dress to wick away the moisture. Standing, I avoid eye contact with everyone giving me sad eyes in the room, especially *his*.

I can't fucking believe the audacity of that man to bring his fucking whore to my mom's funeral.

On shaky legs, I pass Pastor Dave; he gently squeezes my shoulder and takes his place beside his wife.

Standing at the podium, I spread the damp, crumpled paper and smooth it out with trembling hands. Some of the pen strokes are smudged and illegible.

I grip the edges and clear the lump in my throat. There's a chip missing in the wood just off to the left of the paper. I know that area is where Pastor Dave slams his fist down while holding a pen while delivering some of his more passionate sermons.

I pick at it while the silence of the room booms in my eardrums.

"My mom is the grea—" I choke on the word, "was. She *was* the greatest person I've ever known. Pastor Dave described Mom in spades, but she was so much more than her church work." I lift my gaze to the crowd and laser lock on the mistress.

"She was so beautiful, inside and out. She was such a pure soul. She had one true romantic love in her life, and he tore apart our family by," I gesture my hand to the whore, who at least has the wherewithal to look mortified, "fucking his assistant." Gasps fill the room, murmurs bounce off the wall, and Charlene hits Pastor Dave's arm, telling him to do something. I keep him in place with a glare.

I speak a little louder to be heard over the outrage, "Despite dealing with such utter disrespect from the one person who vowed to love and cherish her for all their days, she held her head high. She never let me see the devastation that the selfish bastard caused her. She carried that through until the very end." I fist the paper and crumple it beyond recognition before throwing it at his feet.

"And *that* was a great fucking woman you never deserved, and I hope you two," I point, accusing between the pair, "have the life you deserve." I point at her, "I hope your tits sag beyond surgical repair and your hair thins to the point of bald patches."

I swing my destructive ire back to my sperm donor, "And you. You sorry excuse for a man. I hope the blue pill never works for you and she leaves you for your protégé. He's married with two young children, but we already know that doesn't matter, does it?"

"That's enough!" Dad bellows as he thrusts himself off the pew.

I stomp in his direction and shove him in the chest, "It'll never be enough. I hate you. I never want to see you again. Pack up your Tuscaloosa Barbie and leave." I ignore all the commotion around me and head towards Mom's car.

Well, I guess my car now.

* * *

The smoke sits heavily in my lungs as I tap the cigarette to clear some ash. I blow out the smooth mint as a body collapses on the curb beside me.

"Charls, I'm trying really hard to let you work through your shit. But what just happened in there," she gestures behind us in the vague direction of the church, "was on a whole new level, and now you're smoking? You hate smoking."

I take another drag of the cancer stick. Yes, I get the irony.

I slowly let the smoke flow out of my mouth, drifting on the breeze before disappearing into the ether.

"I hate him for what he did to her, Savs."

She sighs and leans her head on my shoulder.

She's silent for a long time.

"I know. Me too." she finally says.

We sit shoulder to shoulder, head resting on head, and watch as the crowd starts to ebb from Mom's new resting place.

I couldn't bring myself to stand with *them*, so I sat on the curb just outside the cemetery's iron gates.

The final words being spoken on my mother's behalf mean nothing to me.

I knew her. I watched her decline. I heard her last words. These are a bunch of acquaintances at best, except for Mary, of course. That woman is an angel, and we are so lucky to have her and Savs in our lives.

I stub out the cigarette on the asphalt, vowing mentally to throw the butt away. I will never be that inconsiderate person to litter this crap.

"Are you coming home with us? Your dad—" I stop her short by shooting her a death glare at the term.

She holds her hands up in surrender, "Sorry, 'sperm donor', told my mom he would be taking you back to Alabama."

I let out a very unladylike snort, "He's high as a fucking kite if he thinks I'm going to live with him and his concubine. I'm eighteen. He doesn't get a say where I live. Mom sorted stuff out with Mary a while ago that I would stay with you, and that's what I'm going to do."

"I love you, Charls, and you know I always have your back one hundred percent. But.. Do you think maybe you should try to talk to him? He's the only parent you've got left." she whispers the last part sadly.

I know that.

Logically, I know that. But in my heart, he died the moment I found out what he did to our family. If he so easily threw us away, he doesn't deserve my loyalty and respect. The fact that he let my mom lie so he could keep face and keep playing this 'good guy' role makes me fucking sick.

How dare he. I don't need him. He gets zero say moving forward. I will never speak to him again. I wish it were him in that grave instead of her. So...

"No."

Savvy lets out a resigned breath, "Okay. Let's get out of here."

Chapter 46

Fuck me, this shit is fantastic.

I release the Minnie straw as the euphoric feeling feeds my veins. My eyes flutter shut as my head lolls backward on the couch.

A gentle buzzing tickles my thigh, my hand too heavy to reach for the phone, so I let it go until it stops.

The sounds of the house party drift in and out of focus like a movie playing in the background in slow motion.

Everything is dull, sights, sounds, feelings... and I fucking love it.

It's been a month since I lost her. One fucking month.

Buzz.

And again, I ignore it.

My sperm donor showed up at Mary's two days later and begged to speak to me. I refused and sent him on his merry way back to his perfect life with his replacement family.

Oh yes, little Miss Secretary has a kid from a previous relationship. I'm finally going to have that sibling I always begged my mom for. Cue internal eye roll.

Buzz.

Hot breath floods my ear, "You gonna answer that Astra?" his words may be playful, but his tone is anything but.

My mouth is too heavy to open, I simply shake my head without opening my eyes.

Buzz.

I feel the cool air from the absence of the phone.

"Zach," he states flatly.

I knew it was him or Savvy… again.

I manage a "Hm."

Buzz.

His hand latches on my thigh in a painful grip.

Buzz.

He presses the phone directly to my core, and the next buzz has an accidental groan leaving my throat.

"That's right, baby, we are gonna have some fun tonight," he warns before shouting, "Ain't that right, boys?"

Well fuck… time for another line.

* * *

"Fuck!" I whisper shout as I slam my kneecap into the bed frame, "Shh!" I giggle when I realize I'm shushing myself.

"What the fuck? Charls?" a sleepy Savvy sits up on her bed, rubbing her eye.

"Shh, yeah, I'm me," I let out another giggle.

A small bright light illuminates the otherwise pitch black of the room, "Jesus Christ, Charls, it's 4 am. Where the fuck have you been?"

I unbutton my jeans and slide them down, stepping out of the pile and promptly falling sideways into the mattress edge, "Whoopsie."

Using all my efforts to crawl up off the floor onto the bed, I sigh contentedly as my muscles relax into the memory foam.

The darkness is begging for me to join it. I close my exhausted eyes and let out a big exhale.

"I'm worried about you, Charls." Savvy whispers.

I let out a big yawn and pull some covers over my body, "Don't be. I feel great."

If she gives a response, it falls on deaf ears as I drift off to sleep.

Chapter 47

"Fuck, you feel so good." I moan out while rocking my body back and forth across his lap. I can feel his perfect hardness even through our jeans.

His big hands cradle my back as his tongue invades my mouth over and over.

The panting and groaning between us has me desperate to feel all of him, finally.

"Please, Zach, I need you. Please." I implore, pleading the words onto his kiss-swollen lips.

He doesn't respond, but his hands slide from my back to my ass, and he lifts me up, wrapping my legs around his waist.

He flips our positions and lays me down gently on my bed.

I broke down the first time I returned to the house two weeks ago.

Mary had offered to come clean things up and pack up Mom's stuff, but I begged her not to. The only concession I made was that she could take the trash out, do the dishes, and clear the fridge.

Everything looks the same. Smells the same.

The afghan on the couch is thrown haphazardly on the side like it's ready for her to claim it once more at any moment.

But nothing will ever *be* the same. Not her, not me, and not this house.

He starts kissing down my body, lifting my shirt so he can reach my bare skin. His hand follows the path before him until he reaches my center. He rubs me gently over the material.

I need more.

I claw at his shirt, lifting and tugging the hem. He laughs and pulls away long enough to remove it. His warm, tanned, chiseled chest greets me, and I immediately put my mouth on it. I want to mark him, make him mine.

He groans and starts to unbutton my pants. I lift my ass so he can slide them off with ease.

His kisses resume, and he plants one on each hip bone before thumbing both sides of my underwear and sliding them off.

I pull him back up and attack his mouth while reaching for his button. We both fumble a bit, his big body trying to remove his pants without removing his lips. He flings a foil package beside us. Its crinkle sounds like a mass alert to the world that something dirty is about to take place here.

We both laugh as he rolls it on and settles between my legs.

He pulls back slightly and frames my face, "I've wanted you from the moment you walked into those woods, Little Bit. You tore my world apart and set my soul on fire. I didn't know if we'd ever get here, but I had hoped like hell we would." He leans down and places a featherlight kiss on my lips. "I-I love you, Charlotte." With those words, he plunges forward, removing the last barrier between us.

I think that was the first time he's ever said my name.

* * *

I swipe the residue from my library card onto the side of my jeans and rub it off with my hand.

Placing the Minnie straw over the powder, I lean down with one finger covering my left nostril and inhale the whole line.

A knock sounds on the door, and I drop the straw, "Shit." I mutter while wiping the strands of hair off the plastic.

"Charls, get your ass out here. We gotta leave for the airport in three minutes!"

I can't believe it's getting real. My best friend is finally getting to start her dream. I couldn't be more proud of her.

One of us should have a good, happy life. I'm glad it's her. I would give up every moment of happiness that I may find if it meant she got them all.

Mary has agreed to let me stay here even after Savvy leaves for UCF.

I quickly wipe away the white substance on the counter and wash my hands. "Coming!"

I rarely look at the girl in the mirror anymore.

My eyes find my reflection. My cheekbones are sharper than they used to be.

My hair is in an unintentionally messy bun.

My previously vibrant, chocolate irises now dulled down to a drab color.

I study the very faint but clear finger marks on the side of my neck. The ones I convinced Savvy that Zach gave me consensually.

I hate lying to her, but it seems to be all I've done lately.

It's for the best that she's leaving. I know she'll be living her best life.

Just like I know that she'll be better off without me.

I dry my hands on the white hand towels, running my fingers

over the little roses stitched on the bottom. I remember when Savs made these in Home Ec. Just like everything else she does, she crushed that class and could have probably taught it better than Ms. Greene.

I open the door to my very nervous, overly stressed, but beaming bestie.

I wrap my arm around her shoulder and pull her tight against me, "Okay, Savs, let's get you off to your happily ever after, shall we?"

Chapter 48

"Astra! Get your fucking ass in here!" Priest yells from down the hall. I'm so fucked up. My body feels like it's embedded in this couch.

It would take a feat of the utmost strength to get me up.

"What? Can't you just yell whatever it is from there?" I whine.

I flinch when I hear something bang against the wall, most likely his fist.

"Girl, if you don't bring your ass in here..." he warns, and a cold shiver runs through my body, "I promise you won't fucking like it if I have to drag you in here myself."

I fight off the feeling of sinking in quicksand and force myself forward. I stumble a bit, grabbing onto the coffee table for stability.

My blurry eyes blink rapidly to clear the room around me.

Priests' trailer isn't that bad for a bachelor's trap house. It definitely has no womanly touches anywhere. But it's clean-ish.

The man will sell drugs to kids, but he draws the line at shoes on his carpet.

For real, I've seen him pull a gun out and press it to someone's forehead who broke his cardinal rule. Bet he never makes that mistake again.

"Astra! I ain't asking again," he shouts.

I get moving down the hallway and stop in the shadow of his bedroom door frame.

He's standing over his bed with a metal tray in one hand and laying a hand towel down with the other.

The contents of the tray turn my stomach.

A vile.

A long rubber tourniquet.

A very intense-looking needle.

What the fuck?

I open my mouth to speak, but my body trembles so much that I can't make the words come out.

His eyes snap to mine, and he impatiently gestures with his head for me to come in.

I grip the door frame so hard I hear a small snap.

"W-what is t-that?" I shakily question as I cautiously enter the room.

He ignores my question, "Sit down."

I can't take my eyes off the tray. I do not want to shoot up any kind of drug. That's my hard line, and Priest knows it.

His gorilla paws latch onto my bicep, and he yanks me to the head of the bed before shoving me down. "I said fucking *sit*." he snarls at me.

I press my back against the headboard. Hoping and wishing with everything I have that I will melt into the furniture.

"Let me tell you what's about to happen. I had a buddy help me design a new form of AstraMallum. H is still hitting the streets hard, and I need to be competitive. I'm going to need you to help out with this, you understand?" It's a question but not a question. He expects my obedience, always.

I press my lips together tightly, "Priest. You know I don't fuck with needles. We've talked about this before. Why can't you do it? Or get Rick or Bennie?"

His dark eyes lift to mine. He sets the tray down gently and stalks over to me. Fuck, I gulp and press myself as far as I can into the headboard.

He leans down until we are nose to nose. His gorilla paw locks onto my neck, squeezing tightly. My airway instantly cut off.

"Listen here, you stupid little cunt. You will hold your arm out for me. You will tap a vein. And you will shoot this shit up this useless fucking body," his grip tightens, my hand flying to his wrist, trying desperately to release the pressure. It's a fruitless battle; I'm so much weaker than he is.

"If I have to call someone over to hold you down while I do it myself, that can be arranged."

"P-please. No." I plead. But Priest doesn't listen... he never does.

Buzz.

A tear leaks from my eye as I resign to my fate. One way or another, this is happening; how violent is up to me. At least I have a choice... yay me.

The moment the drug enters my body, I know something isn't right.

It feels as though every vessel in my body is beginning to explode. My heart begins to dull to a slow thud, harder than I've ever felt before. Fire is flowing through my veins. My stomach starts to cramp, more painful than any period.

Buzz.

My gaze darts rapidly around the room and lands on Priest. He's sitting in a chair in the corner, watching me with no expression on his face. Studying my reaction. That's all I am to him; a test subject. He doesn't give a fuck what happens to me.

A vise is gripping my lungs as my breaths become stuttered and shallow.

Buzz.

"Fuck. What a waste."

My eyes involuntarily roll, and my head slumps into the headboard. I try like hell to make my brain tell my arm to move, but nothing is happening.

The cramping is so intense I think I may throw up.

Buzz.

I hear an earth-shattering bang, and my body doesn't react. It can't. My body is no longer mine.

Momma, I think I'm coming for you.

That's it. Lights out.

Afterword

Thank you for joining me on this roller coaster ride that has been the beginning of Charlotte's journey. This was an incredibly difficult story for me to write, as much of Charlotte's turmoil came from some of my own life experiences. I am incredibly thankful for the love and support I have around me—especially for my own high-school sweetheart, who has carried me through some of the darkest times of my life.

A huge thank you to all who Beta and ARC read for me and gave a newbie a chance!

The journey doesn't stop here. Buckle up, buttercups. It gets rough.

See you in book two!

Ready to dive into the rest of the series?
Book 2- I Hear You, Charlotte
Book 3- I Choose You, Charlotte

Join my Facebook reader group for all things Charlotte, sneak peeks, and ARC sign-ups.
I See You Coralee- Reader Group

Follow me on Social Media
TikTok @coraleetaylorauthor
Instagram @coraleetaylorauthor

Signed copies are available on my website
www.cltaylorbooks.com/store